Praise for *The Death of the Cyborg Oracle:*

"When I read through *The Death of the Cyborg Oracle*, I wept. Not from sadness, but from its comforting familiarity and universalism during our times of chaos, anxiety, destruction, and uncertainty. Jordan A. Rothacker's treatment of themes ranging from science fiction to religion, and mythology to ontology provides hope in a time of despair, and a call for rebirth and regeneration while we stare at the possibility of our own dystopian future. Most of all, *The Death of the Cyborg Oracle*—through its stunning prose and flow—calls on us to examine, understand, and utilize the past to work for a better present."

— Adam Shprintzen, historian, *The Vegetarian Crusade*

"A bristling archetypal drama, Jordan Rothacker's latest science fiction, is a mythopoeic delight, a space oddity in an asteroid belt of Ovid, Lovecraft, Sophocles, and hip detective stories. A total blam-blam!"

— James Reich, author of *The Song My Enemies Sing*

"*The Death of the Cyborg Oracle* is as much Rabelaisian farce as it is a heart-aching death note to our philosophical and spiritual future. Rothacker's handling of the genre is inspiring, he writes with passion, style, and pathos. I'm convinced he can do anything. Michael Moorcock would have been proud of this book."

— Chris Kelso, author of *I Dream of Mirrors* and *The Dregs Trilogy*

"A solar noir intrigue, complete with climate apocalypse, capitalism abandoned, and the murder of the Oracle at Delphi. Rothacker's bold intelligence and fleet styling will elevate and mesmerize you. Simultaneously a thrilling page turner, and a brilliant critical inquiry as to our time and our future. Smart, creative, prescient."

— John Reed, author of *Snowball's Chance* and *All the World's a Grave.*

"A deeply satisfying, intensely flavored stew of ancient myths and Hebrew iconoclasm, served warm in a glass postmodern bowl. I found it very comforting, especially in its humane account of genders and gods. If this is the future, we don't do as badly as we deserve."

— Peter Gardella, religion scholar, author of *Innocent Ecstasy* and *American Civil Religion*

"With an encyclopedic knowledge of religion, Rothacker takes readers on a noir quest flipped on its head—full of sincerity and hope—that has all the fun of a Rick Riordan book without the teenage hubris. In the domed post-apocalyptic City (which just so happens to save all the best parts of contemporary hipster Atlanta; Crystal Blue or The Earl, anyone?) religion has become a sincere re-enchantment that could potentially save us after all— now that it's divorced from capitalism and group worship. As an artist, I couldn't help but feel simultaneously proud and irked by Rothacker's spot-on analysis of my fictional future artist brethren (I guess some things never change...) clinging to the last vestiges of irony by choosing to genuinely worship fake gods of literary invention instead of the classical gods of world religions, and raucously debating with lead detective Thinkowitz Rabbinowitz at the Variety Playhouse deep into the Little Five Points' night—still weird after 300 years."

— Vivian Liddell, artist, Assistant Professor of Painting and Drawing at the University of North Georgia, host of *Peachy Keen* Podcast

"Rothacker's fresh take on ancient symbolism, cutting characters, and doomsday clock-like cadence strikes a death chord from genesis to cessation."

— Hillary Leftwich, author, poet, and founder of Al·che·my Author Services

"Despite the murder of the titular cyborg oracle, the domed city of Jordan Rothacker's novel seduces you with its post-capitalist, pan-theist society. There has been catastrophe here—environmental, religious, monetary—but this version of a future Atlanta, unlike Philip K. Dick's San Francisco, emerges as somewhere that you might actually want to live. It's a perfect backdrop for a noir that's as inspired by the futuristic as it is the ancient, traversing realms of both the sacred and the profane."

— Farooq Ahmed, author of *Kansastan*

"*The Death of the Cyborg Oracle* is a finely-crafted work of futurist-noir that utilizes the genre as a lens to address society, philosophy, religion, and human nature."

— Peter Woods, cultural organizer & Accomplice

"Rothacker's *The Death of The Cyborg Oracle* is wildly creative, transgressive, and hilarious. With its dystopian futurism, dual critiques of capitalism and Christianity, the book feels beamed in from the future."

— John Vanderslice, musician, producer, *Pixel Revolt*

"Rothacker conjures theology, philosophy and mythology into a cyber noir detective story. Once I got acclimated to post-apocalyptic Atlanta I was all in."

— Don Chambers, musician, visual artist

"When the Profane prophet Alfred North Whitehead made that comment about footnotes and Plato, he could not have foreseen that *The Death of the Cyborg Oracle* would be the ideal embodiment of Platonic mythmaking. Set after the destruction of one Amazon and the dismantling of another, Rothacker's prescient fiction laments and celebrates our all too human blindnesses and insights. Like the eagle-like eyes of Detective Rabbi Jakob "Thinkowitz" Rabbinowitz, it felt like this book was reading and writing me all at once. Its particular mix of knowing tragedy and anarchic hope will continue to resonate long after closing its pages, like the thud of realization made by a brick of marble thrown into the hole of Tartarus."

— Minus Plato, author of *No Philosopher King: An Everyday Guide to Art and Life under Trump* (AC Books 2020)

"Jordan A. Rothacker has written a holy lamb in wolf's clothing with this short novel—on the surface we have a futuristic detective yarn centred on a gruesomely violent murder, but at its heart it's a treatise on the destructive power of unfettered capitalism and the redemptive magic of faith on both a personal and community level."

— Matt Neil Hill, writer, Invert/Extant press

"In a time when we are all pickled in these moments and days, Jordan Rothacker's engrossing work allows us to imagine a world beyond this one."

— Kelly Girtz, Mayor, Athens, Ga

"We would be remiss if, in the sci-fi genre, we did not write about faith. Gods require speculation and innovation, and Rothacker has pulled that off in *The Death of the Cyborg Oracle*, making detectives of the faithful."

— Pam Jones, author of *The Joyful Mysteries*

THE DEATH OF THE CYBORG ORACLE

JORDAN A. ROTHACKER

SPACEBOY BOOKS

Denver, Colorado

Published in the United States by:
Spaceboy Books LLC
1627 Vine Street
Denver, CO 80206
www.readspaceboy.com

First printed November 2020

ISBN: 978-1-951393-04-5

Dedicated to the future, I'm sorry for the past...

And also dedicated to the memories of
Daniel Chameides, Curtis Vorda, Nikki Massey,
Damien Schaefer, Jeremy Ayers, Okla Elliott,
Justin Wilcox, Raymond Langley, West Price,
Kenneth Rothacker, Joan Lee, Nicholas Graves,
and Lisa Rutkin

Future Legend

After ten years in Profane Homicide my transfer to the Sacred Homicide Division of City Safety had been approved, and under the title of Assistant Detective I was finally able to work with Detective Rabbi Jakob "Thinkowitz" Rabbinowitz.

Since my days at the academy I'd studied his cases and life from afar—an infant brain-damaged from a crack in the Dome, a youth of perseverance and study, an early graduate of both City Yeshiva and the Safety Academy, and due to his remarkable physical tenacity, the perfect candidate for one of the first admissions to the SunSpot Cyborg Program—and now as his partner I was excited to witness his mind and methods firsthand.

This turn of fortune in life has given me something to write about for posterity and for you, the future.

Our first case together was to begin immediately after introductions and before I could even settle into our shared pod. Through the carbonite threshold I passed, noting the ancient-looking mezuzah, and was shuffling my box of personal items to access a free hand to shake with that of the august man himself when the Captain approached.

"Thinkowitz, meet Assistant Sacred Detective Edwina Casaubon. Casaubon meet Sacred Detective Rabbinowitz. You call him Sacred Detective Rabbinowitz. You're new. You can call him Thinkowitz when you're not new. You will not know when that is.

"This is a whole other world from Profane. You paid your dues, you handled some good cases, but to the Sacred Detectives around here you're just a highly decorated crossing guard. Nothing wrong with that, we need crossing guards, but Sacred is a whole other world. I can't stress that enough. And put your things down already, you've got a call. But really, he's got a call. You've got a learning experience," said the Captain.

He touched up a preliminary report to the screen on the pod wall and walked out.

I put my box down and exhaled the bubble of anxiety I held along with it.

Thinkowitz wore a black fedora, a long black overcoat, and had a long black beard to match. He turned his eyes from the Captain and put them on me. They were so sharp and intense, like that of an eagle, honing right in on me. It felt like they were reading me and writing me all at once. But then their corners smoothed, tight crevasses relaxed away, and I felt something that I would grow to understand as a welcoming tenderness.

He spoke calmly through an emerging polite smile that could only be described as funereal.

"Take a look at the screen, Casaubon. We're off to see the Oracle at Delphi."

Time... His Trick Is You and Me

You are the future.

Every you ever written to is the future.

I write in the past tense (normally) about my present for you, the future. For you everything is past. My present is your past. Your present is unknown to me; I have only my past for comparison. My past is part of your past. Karma is a bitch.

Our world is domed. Our past was doomed.

This great domed city—and its metropolitan environs —has an elected leader, the City Sovereign. He works for us. And we help him help us. He makes laws with a City Council at our behest and with our consent. It is a legal framework that he is both within and without.

From what I've read, it's not too different a system than what has come before.

City Safety is divided into two thematic jurisdictions: Profane and Sacred. Each has its own divisions. Sacred Homicide covers all sacrificial, metaphysical, and spiritually suspicious deaths.

I'm writing to you, the future. I'm writing because what I've learned from my study of history is that nothing is ever stable, nothing lasts.

We have made our remaining selves safe from the crimes that we have committed. Trust us that we have paid.

A domed city is a city of pylons. Maybe you have found a way around the pylons. Maybe you know them well. Maybe you have found a way to help heal the earth from the cancer that is humanity as we are healing ourselves from that cancerous god.

Living in the Shadow of Vanity/ Dead God with a Kapital K

We are heart-stricken by what we have done.

We all know it. We all feel it.

Every.

Single.

One.

Of.

Us.

Heart-stricken.

While I didn't live through it, I've inherited it. We all have. The inherited trauma of the Katastrophe is an inseparable part of who we are now. That trauma has left a chemical mark on all of our genes, not a genetic mutation, but epigenetic. This explains, on a biological level, the deep loss of faith we all have in that now-dead god, Kapital.

He is gone. Dead. Dead and gone.

And He was very much a he, toxic and many-armed.

From what I've read of the past, specifically that arrogantly declared "Modern World," under that grossly-colored god, Kapital (green in that contemporaneous parlance, red in the bloody damage it wrought, and translucent in its true amorphous and mercurial power), people were far more concerned with secrecy and covetous of privacy. Our society is structurally open.

I'm happy where I am, but sad about how I got here.

Any state sanctioned under that terrifyingly pearline god—I imagine it like a crystal ball that shows everyone what they want to see for a price and looks back into the viewer like Nietzsche's abyss, but not benign, targeted, learning more about you than it showed, all so it can sell your dreams you never knew you had back to you, forever a prisoner of this cycle—can only see its citizens as consuming objects and secrets were a last untouched market.

We traded them all away too; willingly for a commemorative t-shirt. It is a wonder that that god is dead. The only truly dead god, we now know. Everyone is too disgusted that we once believed, and too disgusted to believe again. He died with our shame. He died because we believed so deeply, so completely, we followed him to the precipice and many of us went over, millions, billions... the seas rose, the air became as fire, and finally together we buried Kapital and then raised the Dome upon the pylons together. We have been together ever since. Truly together, open and bare.

Heart to heart, wound to wound. One and the same.

Kapital testified before us all and plead guilty. Profane Prophet Marx merged with Profane Prophet Nietzsche. Kapital is dead and gone. Every other god has been reborn. Every other god has filled our need for belief. From the heart wound comes devotion.

We engage in trade. We have commerce. It is at once social and consensual. It is regulated by us and for us, holistic with City goals. Any capitalism is passive, not active. We have decoupled deservedness from work. The feeling of greed is now the feeling of nausea, migraine headaches, muscle aches, an uncontrollable bowel, a body in duress.

We saw green, we saw red, and we went mad in Kapital's gilded temple.

The victory over that mercurial terror is a somber one. It's hard to rejoice when over half the world is drowned, burned, or starved. It is hard to live on a planet grown hostile, where we feel like unwanted guests.

Our new hope was born from a somber victory, but now finds a range of exalting expression. In the past, it would've been known as socialism. It wouldn't work if we weren't heart-stricken. Sadly, we were ready.

Where once technology was used for mediated displays of audacious virtue and emotional exhibitionism—cattily scoffing at each other drenched in hypocrisy—we now put it all out there and applaud.

We bear it. We wear it. An open society of somber hope.

Our Domed world, built on and in protection against the hot ash and air of Kapital's implosion, houses every possible expression of hope; and hope is expressed through belief.

Our last single, monolithic, communal, state-endorsed belief almost killed us all. We need to believe. The great god Kapital is dead. No more imperial monotheism. We are all henotheists now. Our minds are as open as our society.

Computational technology has developed purely with our needs. From what I have studied it was a brutal weapon in the many grubby green hands of Kapital.

Today it is a supplicating handmaiden to everyone and every god in the City. We have made domed-life possible through it. We failed together to make this possible. The dome itself signals that we fail as we grope together to prevail.

After the Katastrophe we fail together, and we rise again—RESURGA—always ever again through Somber-Hope. Early Domes leaked. We are now thirty years leak-free. Somber-Hope followed the secure Dome and the development of the Sun-Spot Cyborg Program is a sign of how we continue to fail better. We are abundant and it is shared.

RESURGA is our motto.

RESURGA is the City.

In the Villa of Ormen (The Revealer of All Men)

We took the tram to Midtown, traveling mostly in silence.

I followed his lead and answered directly and with brevity the few questions he asked me.

We got off on Peachtree Street a block away from our destination.

The house was a tall rectangle painted black, rising from a stone one-story foundation with steps up the center—an architectural style I knew to be from the early 20th century. Gray light shimmered up and down the corners of the building denoting the parameters as it sat in the middle of a row of more recent towering buildings. This relic carved its own space into our future.

Two uniformed Safety Officers waited at the bottom of the steps, another at the top by the front door.

The illumed marquee read:

Floors 1 & 2
Tartarus, Undertaker

Floors 3 & 4
Shrine of Delphi, Oracle: Tiresias Pythia

It was wrong to be excited since death awaited inside —a human no longer living and breathing, a sight it took me a long time to get used to—but already this new position was different from anything I had experienced in Profane.

I had worked a few cases into the City, but Profane Homicide operated mostly in the suburbs.

Out in the suburbs, ancestor-worship and household gods abound, and even some communal congregations exist. But here within the shadows of so many towers, carbon and chrome touching the limits of our sky, the

City teems with personal gods, the more obscure the better. Communities form out of various shared mythos and overlapping pantheons as people go it alone together. There was too much for anyone to keep up with, and the Profane Homicide wing of City Safety stayed in its own lane. And mostly the suburbs.

But everyone knew of the Oracle of Delphi. Their abilities and reputation for reliable prognostication was sung far and wide. They was esteemed even by those who didn't worship Apollo or any god of Olympus. I was uncomfortably excited and regretted that this was how I would first encounter the Shrine. I had no idea even where it was before and now here I was entering with Detective Jakob Rabbinowitz, my new partner.

"So, the Shrine of Delphi is over an undertaker?" I asked as we moved through the front door and passed a sign for the office of Tartarus.

"Would you have it any other way?" Thinkowitz frowned at me in such a way that I could only understand as condescending or sardonic. I couldn't yet tell. I had studied for this for years and I needed to prove it.

Up the stairs we ventured to the third floor and within the foyer of The Shrine of Delphi we found an austere waiting room of cold, gray, stone tiles. It was like an immaculate cave. Two women waited on a wooden bench. It was clear that both had been sobbing. A uniformed City Safety Officer standing by the bench approached and led us to a panel in the wall that I wouldn't have noticed if he hadn't opened it. He entered a touch-up command to open the stone entry wall.

I followed Thinkowitz into a dark new world.

It's Not Eden, But It's No Sham

Beneath my feet were black serpents.

Long fish or eels, darting, nipping, agitated at each step. They slithered and swam just under the floor, images touched up by my boots, in a shallow sea of dim digital light. It was the only light I could see by. It rose up from illusive depths creating an ivory corona around me and then each step. There was one around Thinkowitz too, but that was it, the only light, and it was personal. I couldn't see more than a foot beyond myself except for the glow around the steps my new partner took.

I followed into darkness with each step before new light.

He stopped, and when I stood next to him, our shared coronas illumed an altar before us.

The darkness beyond the altar was cut into hints of a shape. My body chilled and trembled.

"Ok."

Thinkowitz's voice startled me and full light dropped from the ceiling.

Death sat before me. The uniformed Safety Officer stood at our point of entry a light button by his hand. Thinkowitz stared at me.

I looked back at him, trying to understand if he was making a joke or playing a prank on me.

"I needed you to see what a visitor to the Oracle might see. I've been here before."

His seriousness was forthright and kind.

"I'm saddened to return this way," he said. "They was a good person and a true believer. All true belief is sacred. Baruch hashem."

My eyes fell upon the form beyond the altar: head cast back and a bluish-purple hue about the face as in death by asphyxiation; torso down to the altar draped in three quarter coverage by linen, a single right breast hanging out; hands etched with black tattoos of Greek letters, alchemical symbols, and slashes gripped into the altar as if a defensive move to strike back but in the wrong direction.

Suffocation and death-grip.

For a moment I fell out of my professional function into a state of awe. There was a dead body before me, a prophet of a sun god, and before him a living body, a prophet of logic. I rose back out of the moment, postponing the awe for a later savor.

I walked around the altar and looked into their mouth. Shards of teeth sparkled on a darkness. I shined a light from my finger clip and saw the dental litter splayed across a smooth black surface.

"It looks like a stone"

"Tiresias kept an ovular obsidian on their altar during sessions."

"It looks like someone didn't like their reading. Like maybe they were trying to shut Tiresias up."

Thinkowitz used the forensic scanner to determine body temperature and lividity for time of death but it told us nothing we couldn't already tell on our own. This was fresh.

Knowing what the scans would say, my attention was briefly unfocused and vulnerably drawn into the eyes of Tiresias Pythia. Their eyes were opaque, swirling, and milky like one big cataract in each socket. The eyes angled forty-five degrees to a spot on the ceiling, locked into not-seeing the mosaic of a black dolphin cutting mightily through waves of tiny royal blue tiles.

"They was blind?" I asked, instantly feeling elementary.

"Tiresias was born blind and intersexed; born for this life. Their parents gave them the name. By the time of the SunSpot program, Tiresias' destiny was obvious, if not, as the parents believed, ordained. The cyborg enhancements Tiresias experienced simply augmented all of their senses while leaving their eyes untouched. This was the consent of the child as well as the parents. Tiresias could see through a matrix of sense-data experienced with their ears, nose, tongue, and epidermal nerve endings. They could isolate and hear conversations from dozens of yards away and do the same with sensations in the moving air.

"They built a nexus of knowledge from the unseen and out of reach that clearly influenced their prophesying. This has always given great credence to a divine connection while having a pure base in science. This true power encouraged the deep belief in Tiresias that they were meant to serve Apollo, god of light and truth. It also established the reputation that drew so many here for guidance, even for some outside the Greco-mythos. It is to be doubted that this crime is anything less than Sacred.

"As Maimonides tells us in *The Guide for the Perplexed*, 'It must be fully realized that there is necessarily in every human being some aggressive faculty. The force of the aggressive faculty varies like that of other faculties. In the same way this faculty of divination is founded in all human beings, only in different degrees. These two factors, the aggressive and divinatory, must of course be very strong in prophets.'

"I always suspected, and feared, that the end of Tiresias Pythia would be violent."

He ended and looked away. His lecture was done. He knew I knew that the SunSpot Cyborg Program had augmented his mental function to hyper-retention and instant-accessibility of any and all acquired knowledge. The mind of Thinkowitz was an almost encyclopedic source for religio-mythic knowledge. Everyone at City Safety knew this. And everyone knew how far this sickly child came on his own before the cybernetic adjustments. I couldn't read him but maybe he was shy about his mind.

"I'm going to look around," he said.

"To see what isn't there?" I asked.

"Yes," he said with a soft smile.

His childhood perseverance, achievements, and later enhancements are just a little of what we learn about Sacred Detective Jakob Rabbinowitz at Safety Academy. Mostly we focus on his methodology: Negative Deduction. As with the same argumentative stance through which he described his ancient people's god, Yahweh, Thinkowitz approached investigation through the same process of negation.

To study his methodology, I had to study the theology of his faith. While what is also called apophatic theology was used to deny—as apophatic indicates—anything about Yahweh that wasn't transcendent and unknowable, it also uncovers that god's immanence and knowability. Potential clues at a crime scene aren't limited to what is there, but also what isn't there. This deductive interplay between paradoxes reaches all the way into motives and the identities of the perpetrators themselves.

As he moved about the room in a dignified posture, scanning, I moved at my own rounds. When our orbits briefly overlapped, I heard a mumbling from him. At first, I thought it was Hebrew. And maybe it was, but the melody was familiar. It's strange that I would be shy about hero-worship, but I chided myself for being distracted from my work by my hero's methodology. Nothing I had ever read mentioned a prayer or song Thinkowitz would recite while investigating. He was a trained and acclaimed cantor, but what was this? It seemed reflexive; comforting even.

In another passing orbit, a snippet of the melody resounded within me. I felt it and hummed it. I knew it.

It was "Zoo Zoo Jupiter." Everyone knew it. "Zoo Zoo Jupiter" was one of the most popular songs of the late 21st Century. It was by an anonymous artist who went by MAAWAAM who was part of an artist collective in which everyone went by MAAWAAM. The song was about the development of a zoo on the planet Jupiter to completely represent the whole solar system. The zoo is at once shared sovereignty and shared sacrificial prison.

I had no idea when I would be ready to call Sacred Detective Jakob Rabbinowitz by the common nickname, Thinkowitz. But how long must I wait to ask him about "Zoo Zoo Jupiter," if that even was what he was humming?

Distracted, I missed something.

Thinkowitz pressed firmly at a subtle seam on what appeared to me as a solid stone section of wall. It opened out. I followed him to a vertical crossroads. At a hand gesture I waited. Thinkowitz went down and moments later returned.

"It leads out behind the building into an alley. It's empty. Upstairs are Tiresias' apartments."

Thinkowitz called for the Safety Officer to go upstairs and confirm his assumption of absence. The Officer returned and shook his head.

"Casaubon, I do not believe the devotees in the waiting foyer to be implicated in this crime, but they might provide information, even if they do not know what they know. Shall we?"

THE WAY YOU LOVE ME IS FRIGHTENING

We interviewed Astrape and Bronte.

The interview was conducted in the cold stone anteroom of the Delphic Temple.

Astrape and Bronte; lighting and thunder.

I was starting to understand experientially. I had studied Thinkowitz's cases. Read all news reports daily. Walked through this world when I could. Mostly at night. But this was real. They were real and strange and right before me. Observing and listening to Thinkowitz and his process, I waited until after the interview for a greater understanding when he could explain to me the deeper subtexts of identity that City-dwelling believers expressed.

They were thunder and lightning.

Lightning and Thunder.

They owned it. It was who they were. Every part of their presence and presentation evoked the association. From the angular haircut of Astrape, to the booming curls of Bronte. Their clothes, their voices. She was Thunder. She was Lightning. They were Lightning and Thunder.

I had never heard of Astrape and Bronte before. At first, I had just assumed they were their names. Just their names. But in the City, everyone has a god. This area of Midtown was mostly Greco-Hellenic, and anyone who would come to the Oracle of Delphi would be in that mythos. I can't or couldn't have read up on everything. Failure quaked within me. But here they were. Greek goddess avatars, not just venerators but embodiers, of Astrape and Bronte. Lightning and Thunder. Left and Right hands of Zeus.

It seemed like Thinkowitz knew them, but maybe this was just his manner, the comfort, the comport to talk to anyone as if he knew them, that they were all believers, drinkers at separate springs of the same source.

He took them seriously, but I who grew up in a small, suburban community of ancestor-worshipping, nominal christians—always small c, out of guilt, out of sorrow, of the way big C Christianity easily became big K Kristianity as it merged with Kapital, a dual god vibrating in harmony across modernity to all our death—took them initially as a spectacle. An attractive, intriguing, and deeply human spectacle.

I, of this community—small, close, and in the suburbs —always knew there was much beyond me, but mostly I knew shame. Shame at my own little, familial belief.

I studied to transfer out of Profane to Sacred for this freeing feeling here. This feeling that I know nothing and that others can be just as real or realer than I, and narrowness is the true planet-killer and here we are and here I am, a sorrowful-traditionalist of ancestor-worship worship. But *this* is the City and *this* is Somber-Hope.

I was dizzy and I was excited merely standing in the presence of these women.

They were both born with no name, part of this generation of total-free-sacred-development. Their parents called them a multitude of nicknames to cover over the crevasse of official identity until they expressed an inclination of which deity to follow.

Bronte was a thunderer. Astrape brought occasional flashes of brilliant light.

It also makes sense that both their parents were already of a Greco-Hellenic mythos. Astrape's parents were worshipers of Apollo and Artemis respectively, but with genders reversed. Bronte's parents were gender-aligned worshippers of Zeus and Hera, respectively. Both sets of parents having only one child of female gender-persuasion, in the same neighborhood, was the perfect set-up for two childhood friends, unnamed, to grow up to be the dual arms of Zeus: Thunder and Lightning, Bronte and Astrape.

And so, they, gods, goddesses, worshipping through avatarian practice, were still human enough to need the consult of an oracle. And who better, than the Oracle at Delphi. They spoke for Apollo. They spoke for the god of light and truth and reason and so they spoke Truth. And it was still a Truth for Lightning and Thunder. Astrape and Bronte.

After familiarizing himself with them and making them comfortable, Thinkowitz asked the young women basic questions about when they arrived and if things were different than normal. Their appointment was always at noon on Thursday, Zeus' day, for they were his handmaidens, dual hammers of that god. The door to the inner chamber was closed when they arrived signifying that the oracle was in session. When it was time for their appointment the door didn't open. No one came out—but that wasn't strange, sometimes people left through the side exit out the back alley. Thirty minutes past noon, they finally knocked on the door—the oracle never ran late. When there was no response, they opened the door and peeked in. Then they called City Safety.

"Is there anything else you think will help us in our investigation?" Sacred Detective Rabbi Jakob Rabbinowitz asked.

"No," both answered together, in a sorrowful harmony from two separate tonal qualities, one deeply resonant—a sustained low boom—and the other of high staccato sharpness.

It was beautiful and sad.

Astrape swayed gently in her seat with shimmering anxiety. Bronte, the bold thunderer, looked like she was about to explode. Tears ran and stumbled down all four cheeks.

I felt like I understood them. Almost. This place was having an effect on me. Its feeling of sanctity was palpable and borderline converting.

Speed of Life

I looked down on the City and the crowd alive.

We were taking the elevated tram from pylon to pylon away from Midtown in the direction of City Hall.

Where I am from, where I have spent almost my whole life until a few days ago, there is nothing like this, or nothing as much like this. Touched-up color, glowing neon trimming every structure. Touched-up color glowing in twitching movements of digital carbon touch-fabric on every odd person down below. The world glowed in forced color, part of our sullen and Somber-Hope.

This was an accompaniment to the dusty stone-gray starkness of the Temple of Delphi. The outer expression of that inner sanctum.

In and out of the shadows of pylons and buildings, the colorful glows showed life in its most extreme achievement. Each movement, whether glowing or not, was a deific devotee. A believer. A true believer. And each had their own deity.

The ancients—and even moderns—handed us down enough gods and we of this new world were not going to fail them. Nothing immortal dies. We won't let it.

Everyone is pretending and dead serious at the same time. That is how religious devotion in the City has always felt to me.

Without Kapital—that ever-hungry god—there is no worry of appropriation. No one is covetous or wants to kapitalize on religion. People don't believe they possess their god, but that they've acknowledged its veracity and surrender to it. How could one be appropriating if one is confirming a divine reality? It's the kindness, fealty. They do not take on faith; they go under it.

In our Meta-Modern world, Post-Katastrophe, the world of RESURGA, religiously we are content over context. All gods stripped of their context and embraced for their content.

The light gray sky of day was above me through the glass of the Dome, through the glass of the tram ceiling. But I couldn't take my eyes from the life below.

The rapturous awe must have been on my face, seeping through the professional façade cultivated in my ten years in Profane. My new partner must have noticed.

"This Domed world is like a Holy Mountain, Casaubon. There is a prophet in my faith, Isaiah, who is also a prophet in yours, who described such a Holy Mountain, as a place where a lion might live with a lamb, a leopard with a goat, a child with a cobra, and none will harm or destroy another. We have that now, not through a single shared god, but through a single shared dead god. That loud void reverberates still. All true belief is sacred, and our world is covered in true belief as the waters cover the sea."

It's Too Late to Be Late Again

Thinkowitz waited outside.

He was indulging me. Any lead is a lead, even if pursuing one does nothing more than rest my mind.

Doing something, *anything* also helped to rest my mind.

I headed up to the fourth floor of City Hall. The fourth was the floor of Deeds, Records, and History. This is an open society, and that is of course what we have all agreed to; and agree to again at all City Orientation meetings. Material covetousness is such a rare motive for murder. All property is shared and socialized, but some relics of the past exist. It would certainly be a matter for Profane, but I was still covering all possibilities.

At the head of the rotunda, just past the elevators, sat the book/s. In a raised glass case, with perfect lighting, sat the evidence against us. Our indictment. The book/s that show we knew it all and did nothing to stop it. We knew it all and didn't care. We knew it all but couldn't believe it. Didn't want to believe it. Driven mad by Kapital into denying our own biological imperative as a species.

I passed *Carbon Ideologies*, by the Profane Prophet William T. Vollmann, and made myself look at the covers of both volumes—I always made myself look, every time I passed—and headed for the open archive of land deeds.

Under Sacred Sites, the Temple of Delphi wasn't hard to find. The documentation confirmed that the Shrine and Temple were City-Sanctified, under the cooperative ownership of the City Citizens, and under the proprietorship of Tiresias Pythia. There was no indication of the ancient relic of private ownership. Property was no reason to remove Tiresias from their position and this world.

There was nothing more to pursue in City Hall.

Thinkowitz greeted me outside with a thoughtful smile.

"It is maybe true that you have studied up too much on the past, on Pre-Katastrophe motives? Or perhaps this is also a side-effect of ten years in Profane," he asked with a cautious calm and respect.

"It is maybe true, yes. Thank you for indulging me. The ways of Sacred are new to me. I will follow you."

KINGS OF OBLIVION

I heard nothing until the door was open.

And then it was an enveloping chamber of sound. It was music and everything that wasn't music all at once. The arts are as alien to me as an experiential understanding of the sacred. Thinkowitz was my Virgil and every stop was paradisiacal.

The walls were touched-up to be a twitchy Pre-Katastrophe woodland. Thick, fecund, and verdant. Like Botticelli's "Primavera" but itchy and multi-dimensional with light cutting through the leaves and between trunks of trees.

The boys—but really young men or fully-grown youth —moved in manic undulations that froze rhythmically into formal gestures and positions. One arranged and modulated pulses in the ninety-degree parameters established by a touch-wall and a touch-table with board of neon keys. The other held wooden reeds lashed together in descending lengths. They were shirtless and loin-clothed, a mess of wild copper curls on their heads, jagged ginger fluff down all four legs, and the skin of their torsos and faces dappled with freckles like red Georgia clay.

They had buzzed us in but acted as if we weren't there.

"Fennec fox," one shouted, standing free.

The other manipulated tones between the table and wall.

I couldn't tell them apart and they switched positions and roles in composition so quickly it felt like an intentional trick even though they were ignoring us.

"Platypus," the other now shouted in his new place.

My pulse raced and I felt sickly vulnerable. A tone from nowhere tickled the crown of my scalp.

Not just the music, but the movements and pheromones of the young men caused emanations and radiations from physical parts of me connected to sensuality and eroticism; parts deeply feminine.

"Hawaiian honeycreeper," one shouted.

A tone passed through my lower back, beats rumbling and beats churning.

"Pika," now the other one.

A stabbing and a feeling of fire at my coccyx. Sweat budding at my nape.

"Staghorn corral," maybe either, maybe both.

The one who spoke last drew forth the wooden pipes of descending sizes. With the instrument almost at his lips he froze. It was a calculated pose but as the other one at the table stopped with a hand just above the neon board of keys, I realized it was all the result of Thinkowitz raising his hand.

"Detective Casaubon, meet Max and Jack Panic."

"Hello," I shuddered trying and failing to sound official.

"Xaire, Hello," came back in perfect stereophonic harmony. Then "Hello, I'm Jack," and "Hello, I'm Max," from each individually.

As long as they stayed exactly where they stood, I'd know Jack (left) from Max (right).

"What was that?" asked Thinkowitz.

"We call it 'Dead Voices.' The music takes you through all the feelings of being in your skin..." begun Max and Jack finished:

"...And the lyrics are names of Pre-Katastrophe animals now gone."

"How long is it?" asked Thinkowitz.

"We are in our sixth hour today but the longest we've..." said one and the other:

"...Ever performed was fifty-two hours..." said the other and both:

"...There are a lot of dead voices."

"True, this is true. However, you brothers are true artists and your art honors the dead as much as it honors the living who experience it. Casaubon, the last time I saw the Brothers Panic perform at The Earl they recreated a wonderful version of 'Warszawa'."

"The next time we perform we will recreate 'Weeping Wall' just for you."

"Sounds like a mitzvah, thank you! Shalom, my dear friends. But it is with deepest regret that we visit you today in official capacity."

There was a silence in the room that felt truly alien to the environment.

"Tiresias Pythia has been killed," spoke Sacred Detective Rabbi Jakob Rabbinowitz with solemn dignity.

The alien silence knew awkward freedom for just one beat more before the manic panic explosion of two shocked and angered devotees of horned, goat-god Pan.

"It's a crime!;" "...A crime!;" "...A sacred crime;" "...A violation of all that is holy;" "...And sacred;" they both shouted in and out of chorus with movements erratic and violent.

The energy of the room felt like chaos under my skin, a feeling "Dead Voices" had only begun to hint at.

The only thing calm was Thinkowitz. Focusing on him, I breathed better. For another beat he let the brothers rage and then raised his hand again.

They stopped.

They panted like tired animals.

"We are not just here to bring you troubling news, but to ask you questions," said Thinkowitz.

"You don't think we had anything to do with it?" they asked.

"No, I do not. And I am quite sure that if you have been playing 'Dead Voices' for the last five hours the memory for the touch-wall and -table would provide an undeniable alibi. What we would like to know is if there are any reasons why someone would want to kill the Oracle of Delphi?" asked the senior detective.

The feeling of panic that had stirred all the molecules in the room and even seemed to send a program of electric wind through the woodland trees and leaves touched up on every wall began to dissipate.

In their way, they began to explain that Tiresias was so good and precise at prophesying that they brought people towards the Greco-Hellenic pantheon. It would be unthinkable for a worshipper of any related gods to want to harm the Oracle of Delphi. The Brothers Panic both reiterated what everyone knew, that "Killing the messenger won't change the message." Maybe a rival prognosticator from a different mythos could do something like this but that would most like backfire.

"Backfire? How?" I asked.

"All believers are hungry for truth, Casaubon. Everyone is hungry for evidential confirmation of the divine, any divine, and the more specific the better. As news of the Oracle's death spreads many will interpret the murder as a reaction to revealed truth. An occult truth, dark and secret. A truth so shocking that the messenger needed to die. This will only increase the reputation of the Oracle of Delphi and the veracity of Apollo. Killing Tiresias Pythia would do the opposite of discrediting them. It has probably already started. There is a rapid rate of dissemination of information in the City. If the Brothers Panic weren't making 'Dead Voices,' they would've known what happened before we arrived."

"It's true. We ignore all messaging while rehearsing," they said together.

"There is probably messaging from Astrape..." said one of them, and then the other:

"...or Bronte..." said the other, and back to the first:

"...or Daphne..." said the first, and back:

"...or Puck..." said the other, and back:

"...or Tony..." said the first, and back:

"...or Demetrius..." said the other, and:

"...or Egeus..." said the first, and:

"...or Aegis..."

Until Thinkowitz had to once again stop their increasingly energized shouting and gesticulations with a raised hand. They panted and sweated anew.

"Max, Jack, you brothers should return to your music, if you can. There is enough grief in your work already, but expression can help you heal. Please, if you hear anything, bring it to my attention. On behalf of City Safety, and myself personally, we offer sincere condolences."

"Since our Great God Pan is a lover of merry noise, as is Apollo, Tiresias' God..." said one, and the other:

"...We shall tell Anne-Locke and Suzy that in two Saturday's, at our performance..." said the other, and back to the first:

"...We will perform 'Weeping Wall' with respect to you and in..." said the first, and back to the other:

"Tribute to Tiresias instead of selections from 'Dead Voices'."

As an aside to me, Thinkowitz clarified that Anne-Locke was a worshipper of Goddess Echo and manages The Earl, the musical performance center, with Suzy, a worshipper of Narcissus. They are audio and visual.

"That is a wonderful tribute and I am sure your god and their god will appreciate the reverence, for as

Maimonides reminds my people, 'Whoever fails to mourn for a sage will not live long, and whoever fails to mourn for a worthy person deserves to be buried alive'," he told the brothers.

We left and in the few seconds it took for their door to slide shut behind us I could hear the opening pulses and taps of "Weeping Wall" rising up. We rode down in the elevator in silence and then out on North Druid Hills Avenue I stopped and looked toward my superior for guidance.

"The brothers denied a believer could have done this and you explained that a rival prognosticator wouldn't commit such a crime, if not just to avoid the backlash. What if a believer was motivated by the same reason why a rival wouldn't?" I asked.

"That scenario, Casaubon, is not only deeply disturbing, but sadly possible," he replied. "I must think on where we should look next, but first I must say the Kaddish as sunset is soon upon us. Maybe, yes, it is good for you to rest as well? Positive habits are important. Today, I believe, has been a significant day in your development as a newly appointed Assistant Sacred Detective."

He was correct and I agreed openly. I would try to rest.

COLD, COLD NIGHTS UNDER CHROME AND GLASS

At night I like to go out walking in the City.

I've never been particularly good at resting. I'm fine at sleeping, but the rest it takes to get me there is an effort.

The City amazes me and stimulates my whole being. The tips of my fingers tingle as do the follicles of the hair on my head all the way down a nervous follicle path of neck, spine, and forearms.

Now as a detective with Sacred Homicide I needed to better familiarize myself with this place. I tell myself that it is necessary for work, this exercise in rest unto sleep is of a professional interest, and while that is true, I am driven by a deep and strange fascination.

Profane Homicide has jurisdiction in the City—its purview categorical and not geographical—but most of our investigations were out in the suburbs so that's where City Safety kept me. I was born and raised in the suburbs and that's where my family lives still. After all the work and training I felt disappointment in never really leaving home.

Ten years in proximity to my family's home in Roswell allowed me to serve as a good daughter and make regular visits for family dinners. Monitoring the slow, steady aging of elderly parents—poisoned through early Dome development—buoyed my resolve against resentment, but now my time has come, and they will understand less frequent visits.

Now I live *in* the City and maybe one day I will be *of* the City.

There are only few of my faith here. The suburbs are like our catacombs.

Those who have chosen the City, have chosen a self-purgation in sewage, beneath the City, (but far from the filth of ancient Rome ours are clean catacombs of divided irrigation, both water and waste).

I have read that the younger Pliny called christianity "a degenerate sort of cult carried to extravagant lengths." How could he ever know that it would become the state religion of Rome; the atrocities committed in its name over two millennia and more; how it would merge with Kapital into the double helix of Modernity; how a few like my family would try to salvage what could be scraped-off from the charred husk of the dead god with a Kapital K.

We who endure with it know our god is one that dies and is reborn through the failure of humanity, who loves and forgives. Shyly we try to love and forgive ourselves. It's all we can do. One might be crying out in the septic wilderness beneath my feet whenever I walk the streets of this City.

The City fascinates me in the same way as Thinkowitz. They are not so different. Austere and formidable structures that contain the wealth of the world's historic engagement with mystery. That describes both City and Thinkowitz.

That night, after my first new day, rest inside, in my new home, was impossible. There were memorized secular gospels in my head leading me out into the night, and I said to myself:

I am she that walks with the tender growing night, I call to the earth and sea half-held by night. Press close bare-bosom'd night—press close magnetic nourishing night.

Our Profane Prophet, Walt Whitman, gives us a bright light in the darkness of the past to connect us to the human hope behind a new society of parity and sorrowfully/joyfully adjoined differences.

Each individual, its own jagged blade, often with their own unique object of worship, and together, all together, we sway in a Domed, controlled breeze as one united field of grass.

In a Domed and sufficient world, night was a choice, but most still made it. By day these in-town streets and trams teemed and dreamed out-loud and alive. As a mass we melt and meld together. But with the quiet of night, I felt more individual than ever.

I walked north from my new home in East Atlanta. Trams whirred past, by and over. But I needed to feel the nourishing night and I wasn't actually going anywhere.

I took the stairs up to the I-20 elevated park. This greenway cut across the City from western to eastern suburbs. It presented a nice wide gap within rows of towers and pylons to look to the sky unobstructed. Recently, I had found this one perfect spot within trees of pine and elm to look straight up through the crisscrossed pattern of elevated tramlines.

It was late, and there was no Dome-glare, and the stars called down to me in the same way they always have in the suburbs where the towers are lower and further apart and there are no elevated trams.

They reminded me that even though they are far away, so far away that they might be dead already since sending that light, they are not gone. Something remains across millions of light years.

Dead stars give me hope.

Down from the I-20 greenway I walked to Wyman then wound east into Kirkwood. Paths of least resistance. Paths of great resistance. The contours of the earth have never fully bent to our dominion. Pylons stand up on hills and ridges and down in valleys and troughs just the same.

I had gone out at night before in the City, several times, but this felt new. I now live here. I am part of the City. It is mine to engage, mine to behold. Partnered with Thinkowitz, the City is now my beat, our beat, my beat.

Cities were once exalted in the time of Modernity as a home of that one god with a kapital K now long dead. They were exalted as examples of the wonder that we thought ourselves to be. That arrogant wonder is now the shame-shadow under which we all walk and live.

The City excites me now for the same reason it excites everyone who lives here:

THIS IS WHERE THE GODS ARE!

The Aztecs once felt that way about Tenochtitlan. Abandoned by the Maya, it stood empty, a shrieking void of stone and occult passages, waiting for them. What else could it be, but a home of the gods?

Twisting through these mostly empty streets at night, so quiet and cool, around corners of stone, carbon, and titanium can feel as I imagine those occult passages.

In the density of this City by day I could grab anyone and ask, where do you keep your heart outside of yourself? And they would answer with glee, and all somberness aside, I worship Kuhu! or Gueggiahora! or Ninedinna! or whoever transcends this Domed world for them!

At City Safety, I've grown to know an archivist who worships Ninedinna. Ivy Andermatt has merged her role in our world with her worship. She lived in Oakhurst in an area of Sumerian mytho-clustering. Her stories make me feel connected.

But this new night I wandered west at McClendon, not east. I was compelled and directionless at once. Where did I go? It didn't matter. Bare-bosomed night was alive and warm and pressed close.

When McClendon ended into Euclid, I was in the strange little world of Little Five Points, a cluster of buildings left low, a neighborhood almost three hundred years weird. No matter how quiet most of the City is at night, this is one of the places that never was. My heart raced in a way now familiar after the Temple of the Oracle and the home of the Brothers Panic.

Everyone was everywhere. A shimmering, touched-up blur of electric colors and expression all around and above me. Night was a choice not made here.

Crystal Blue to my north was a gallery of geodes and sparkling displays of what the earth had to offer. I passed Criminal Records, a place for music and curios almost as dense as the floor to ceiling gallery of curios and ephemera of distant pasts at Junkman's Daughter around the corner.

At Kerry Thornley's Body Art there was a lively line of people talking and waiting for body augmentation and epidermal imprinting, so I crossed to the other side of the street.

Outside the Variety Playhouse, a gallery for visual and music presentation, I stopped to observe a motley array of people congregating within. Through the windows I saw costumes of ritual display and proudly ostentatious pageantry. Conversations cut loudly across the wide hall. If they were fighting it was with a joyful fury and furious joy.

Off to one side, no less loud, active, or passionate than anyone else, but in his dour, dark suit, was Sacred Detective Rabbi Jakob "Thinkowitz" Rabbinowitz.

SCARY MONSTERS

"I thought you were saying your Kaddish?" I asked him after he stepped out of the Variety Playhouse.

Through the window I had watched for maybe longer than I should have, but I was captivated. I couldn't hear anything, but it was all so intense.

Turning to shout at someone in the crowd standing near the window, Thinkowitz had caught my eye and then smiled. He didn't seem shocked to see me though. He finished what he was shouting before he came outside.

"I did. I prayed penitently and I have glorified my god in remembrance of my friend. And then I went out. Do you expect me to be gnashing my teeth and renting my vestments all night?" He smiled and removed a simple white cotton handkerchief from his inside jacket pocket and dabbed the sweat from his brow beneath the brim of his fedora.

"I don't sleep well, Casaubon. As it is obvious that neither do you. My situation is a little hard to explain, but the clearest I can make it for others is that my mind does not turn off. I will eventually sleep. However, my dreams are also exhausting."

"So, you come to the Variety Playhouse to argue and wear yourself out?" I asked.

"Why, yes. Though initially I just went out to wander. Wherever I wander I wind up somewhere like this. For as Maimonides advises, 'Gather in the homes of the wise who study and teach. Let their abode be your destination, for there you will derive pleasure;' and while this isn't a domicile, it is a home of wisdom and teaching."

I looked back through the glass at a congregation of humans at once different from each other and vastly different from my new partner in appearance.

"You seem confused, Casaubon."

"I'm sorry. I didn't expect to see you here. How do you fit in with them? In there?"

"I am a Jew, a child of Israel, and as a rabbi, a leader and teacher in my small community in Sandy Springs near City Yeshiva. However, being here is very in line with my tradition. We debate. We argue. We make midrash or commentaries. Then we make commentaries on the commentaries. We write back across time like this. And we argue with our contemporaries."

"Yes, but all these worshippers here. They're not Jewish."

"No. Not at all. Do you see the woman in the center of the room with dark stars inked over her arms, sternum, and face, wearing the black shimmering shift of mesh? That is my friend Zoe Aurora and she worships Ammutseba, *the Devourer of Stars*, a dark cloudy tentacled mass that absorbs falling stars.

"To her right towards the wall, in the robe touched-up as a wind-swept ancient Sahara is my friend, Alegria Touchshriek, who worships Nyarlathotep, *the God of a*

Thousand Forms, the Crawling Chaos, the Faceless God, the Stalker Amongst the Stars.

"Alegria and Zoe are arguing cosmic terror in relation to trauma with my friend, Pettyjohn Oddo, they worships Cxaxakluth, an indescribable and amorphous outer god.

"And do you see on the sidelines of the argument, waiting to pounce with a cutting rhetorical device, her black hair slicked down her back and then wrapped and woven around her body? That's Bian An, who worships Ah Pook, *the Destroyer*. I wish I could hear what she is about to retort.

"All of those gods are creations of horror and science fiction writers of the late 19th and early 20th centuries. From Clark Ashton Smith, Lovecraft, even William S. Burroughs."

"So, they are worshipping gods who have never really existed, as in no one ever seriously worshipped them or believed in them before?" I asked.

He laughed. It was the first time—and maybe the only time I can remember—he actually laughed at me. It was a deep laugh in his solar plexus. It came out propelled by his diaphragm and I felt it. I really felt it.

"Casaubon. Our world is," and he gestured widely with his arm, pointing skyward Dome-ward at the center of his arc, "the way it is because most of the planet worshipped a now dead god with a Kapital K and did that god ever *really exist*? Very few even called it a god. We have examples from its late state in the 20th century from Profane Prophet Walter Benjamin to songwriter Trent Reznor, but most humans thought they weren't even being religious."

His soft smile returned and helped return me to a place of acceptance.

"I frequent many diverse homes of the wise who study and teach, with work and in my wanders. Those who frequent such places as the venues of Little Five Points, or the art galleries of the West End, are neo-Modernists in their devotional tendencies and tactics."

"What does a new form of Modernism have to do with worshipping such horrific gods?" I asked. My calm was enhancing, and my mode of mood was turning towards receptive.

"There is a bit of the flagellant here in characterizing their practice of religiosity. Most of these devotees, many of whom are artists, stoke comfort in the uncomfortable. Their practice involves cultivating a feeling of spiritual anxiety. Their gods are utterly indifferent to their humanity. Mighty, fierce, horrifying, and distant. Like the stars many claim their gods came from. Our world is one of connection and warmed with somber joy. And their gods also connect them to an apocalyptic Modern Age of alienation and dehumanization."

He paused for a moment as if to wait for me to catch up, and he was right to. I was hung up on his mention of the stars. Maybe these neo-Modernists also felt hope at the thought of dead stars.

"It is almost utterly the opposite of my god," he resumed. "And this is what I find so intriguing and stimulating. The god of my people works through history and teaches us to survive no matter what happens, whether it's enslavement in Egypt, the Babylonian Exile, the destruction of the Second

Temple, the Inquisition, the Holocaust, or the Katastrophe. Historical revelation leads us to a deeper understanding of hashem and from tragedy we expand our theology. We are a plucky people. This is our territory. We led the way during the RESURGA."

He paused. Lights from inside went off and then back on. I felt like he paused right before the first flicker, but I couldn't remember.

The chatter and furor abated with immediacy.

The first out of the Variety Playhouse was a man far taller than me at five four and even Thinkowitz at six two. His hooded jumpsuit was complete with pine bark, either organic or well-rendered. He stopped at my partner.

"L'chaim, Rabbi!" he said with true joviality.

"Go forth with Ix Tab, *goddess of ropes and snares*! Have a good night, and play safely, Tuck Teal," said Thinkowitz before they embraced.

Next in a tunic that shed an infinite rainbow of glitter and never seemed depleted, her skin a light orange marmalade, a blonde woman my height but of a slighter build stopped.

"Go forth with Yog-Sothoth, *the all-knowing conglomerated spheres out of time*. I wish we could have debated the Sefirot further, my dear Aster Phlox," said Thinkowitz.

"L'chaim, dear Rabbi. Until next time," her words like sensual syrup; and she bowed slightly, raining glitter only upon the toes of my partner's black shoes.

One after another. I stood by and smiled and nodded my head in recognition as almost every single Neo-Modernist to emerge from that crowded space acknowledged Sacred Detective Rabbi Jakob "Thinkowitz" Rabbinowitz as if he was the host of this party. He knew the name and deity of each devotee.

"There is also a selfish reason I frequent homes of the wise who study and teach, although a selfish reason for the common good," my partner said turning to me, alone with him in front of the Variety Playhouse.

It was clear that my role in the dialog of our chance meeting tonight was to wait receptively during his pauses. I was also, finally, exhausted. So, I waited.

"For the ancients, philosophy was profound, and religion was superficial, but also social practical, and necessary. My people can be blamed, at least in the West—or the western side of Asia—for merging the two. True, it is the pitfall of theology but we bring it down to earth with a love of commentary and a consistent living debate.

"Debate and commentary, these cherished traits of my people, while active in the forefront of my mind, help focus the reach and associative connections in the rear. Succinctly, while my mind works, my mind works. I may have discovered an obsidian connection."

"Obsidian connection?" My brows puzzled at him along with my words.

"Go home. Rest is certainly overdue, and sleep is necessary. You have truly learned a great deal today. Allow me to return to Maimonides again with a recommendation: 'When you finally depart from the house of learning, be conscious of what you are taking home with you. Fasten it in your mind and deposit it in your heart.' There is more learning to do tomorrow, Casaubon."

We Are the Dead

"Who are you calling crazy? You're the one talking to a ghost."

He wore a thousand little sheets of digital carbon fabric. Each one was touched-up with a feather. With each random dramatic thrust of his hands—punctuating his words?—he fluttered a shimmering rainbow of color.

I hadn't said anything but hello when I sat down next him at the tram stop.

The night was now cool, gray, and quiet.

"You're the one talking to a ghost," he said again.

Iridescent light trailed the movement of his hands.

For some, the heart-strickens is more than we can take.

When the tram arrived, I left.

I left him behind. The digital carbon fabric was fluffed up and activated like a prismatic bird.

His eyes were wide open and looking at nothing.

When I Live My Dream

I rarely dream.

But I have a reoccurring nightmare.

It's a collectively common nightmare.

We all have it at some point to some degree, as confides my assigned City Safety Grief Counselor. It is not a matter of shame, but we are all shy to talk about it, she explains. The grubby reach of the dead god finds us on the deepest primal level.

I am sitting... there is no color... I know I can stand but I won't allow myself... I am not allowed... I can't stand... everyone is sitting... it's ok, everyone is sitting... billions of us sitting at desks all around me... floors above me... and I know there are those who stand... floors beneath me... standing and they can sit... I know they can... but they don't... they don't want to... and I envy them... I hate them... I hate them so much... may they drown... may they burn... may they be gone... so I can stand... I can take that place... why do they get to stand... they don't deserve to stand... they don't even deserve to sit... I can stand if I want to... why should I have to sit just so they can stand... why should I have to... why should I... but there is no color... the world is black and white... sitting and standing... there is only black and white... why should I have to sit when he gets to hang... a man in a suit hangs from a giant clock outside... why can't I be outside... another man turns from gear to gear... he is inside a great machine and each gear feeds him to another... he doesn't seem to mind and he keeps reaching for his hat... why can't I be inside the machine... the minute hand on the giant clock ticks again and the man hangs on... the man in the gears is inside the clock... maybe he isn't... with a tock the minute hand points down and the man falls... why can't I fall... why does he get to fall... the gears spit the man out... he has his hat now but he is on a wide belt moving, continuously moving... metals arms reach for him, some missing, some poking... men stand aside the moving belt... standing... why can't I be on the moving belt... and as the minute hand ticks back up another man hangs on... as the minute hand rises with a tock I can see that the man's hands are sweaty... there is fear and anguish in his face as *he regrips against the sweat furiously over and over... good, if he falls I can go outside... I can hang from the sweeping minute hand... why can't I have what he has... why must I walk down this hall... such a long hall, yellow flickering fluorescent lights in a drop-down ceiling... one door after another but I can't go in... I know they aren't locked... but I can't go in... why can't I go in... others get to go in... why should I have to walk this hall... I walk forever and I know I'm walking while others don't have to walk... I hate them and want them to burn... to drown... and at the end of the hall... at the end of forever... I come to a door... I wait... I can't go in... that's all I know... others can go in... others less deserving than I... burn... drown... burn... drown... why should I have to...*

I wake up sick and shaking with a fading memory.

The trauma activates all of the body's deepest response functions. My bowels are troubled and loose. I am shamefully aroused with an engorged clitoris and a sticky flood. Thick, bilious vomit crusts the sides of my mouth and pillow.

I worry I might die one day this way.

My assigned City Safety Grief Counselor is dutiful to calm me from this common worry. In our audacious world of spiritual exhibitionism and a boundless zeal for belief we are quiet to this lingering danger. There have been actual deaths from this dream. Those deaths are the domain of Profane.

While we are sheepish and ashamed about them, we will not make them Sacred.

Black Star

"Was obsidian a message or merely convenient?"

That is the question with which Thinkowitz greeted me.

It was something I tried to parse last night reading up on obsidian before finally sleeping. An extrusive igneous rock formed out of volcanic glass not found in the soil here so most likely the purview of collectors.

We were at the thin tree line and both reflexively took a breath of what came from those leaves before heading forth.

In "Rock Garden - F" of Piedmont Park—one of the several green spaces designated for ritual—we found Uco Azul just finishing up.

Within cloths of blood red velvet, he was wrapping stones that looked as dark as a hole in space.

My partner greeted the man cloaked in a rough burlap blanket bearing an image of Tenochtitlan and the sun and announced who we were.

"Oh hey, hi, yeah, Sacred, huh? Real great, real, real great to meet you, Detective Casaubon. And it is a great honor, real, real, REAL GREAT honor to meet you Rabbi, I mean, Detective Rabbinowitz. A lot of respect, you know, proceeds you to me before meeting you here now."

He made an awkward, yet sincere, little bow-type movement. Then he swung the burlap blanket over his head. His groin and buttock were wrapped in papery white linen and the rest of his body was naked before me.

Azul seemed dopey, and overly prone to inebriation, but his body was as serious as I now imagined his devotion to be. Skin, just darker than mine, taut and sinewy everywhere. His rituals must have been intense—or the obsidian heavy—as his muscles were puffed up in his thighs and chest. Even beneath the wrapped linen he was surging. From feet to neck his body was dappled in inky jaguar spots and as he turned to fold the blanket, I saw the pattern was interrupted on his back by a detailed rendering of the sun-shaped Aztec calendar. The sun radiated as back muscles rippled.

I woke uncomfortable and on edge and the body before me was taking me further askew. Thank heavens for Thinkowitz.

"We are here because your collection of obsidian is widely known. It is part of your devotional practice, yes?" asked my partner.

"Yes, yes, oh yes. I commit my life, my blood, my heart, my hands to Tezcatlipoca, the *Lord of the Near and the Nigh*, *He By Whom We Live*, the *Possessor of the Sky and Earth*! He is the smoking mirror, the darkness through which see ourselves for the first time. And ya know, Tezcatlipoca means *smoking mirror*, and that's obsidian. Shit's amazing. So smooth, so dark."

Uco Azul unwrapped a wide and black perfect circle. On blood red velvet it sat like a hole in space.

Thinkowitz and I graciously considered it as he smiled proudly.

"It is very beautiful. I understand why so many different peoples have revered such a stone. Do you gift or trade pieces of obsidian beyond what is actively used in your rituals?" asked Thinkowitz.

"Yes, well sure, but yes, occasionally, but only rarely, yes. It isn't that hard to find though. Crystal Blue, the Phoenix and the Dragon, lots galleries or ritual supply shops have obsidian"

"Tezcatlipoca is a god of sorcery and divination along with being a god of the night and winds, correct?" asked Thinkowitz.

"Yes, sure, yes, and even more, yes. So much more. So much more." He was about to continue with such exuberance but caught himself. "Wait, was there some kinda Sacred crime involving obsidian?"

"Yes, Uco Azul. That is why we are here. Where were you yesterday around 11:45am?" asked Thinkowitz.

"Where was I? When? 11:45? In the morning? I was enhancing my freak next door with my friend Juani

Negra. He worships the Mayan god, Tohi. That god's name literally means obsidian. Juani makes the best belly-burning pulque! We are like mythos cousins! It was our Thursday, midday, mind-away.

"He's real for real coming here any sec. Like in the quick blink of a sec he could be here. Blink, blink, sec, sec. He uses this space too. Friday, when the sun is high. We shine the light upon the stone. Bright, bright, light, light and the stone deepens its darkness. He's returning my macuahuitl that he borrowed too."

And there he was. Walking up over the hill and down towards this clearing. He had a solid frame like Uco Azul but beneath clothing and held a long wooden object that looked like a flattened cricket bat lined in sharp black shiny teeth. As a weapon it looked formidable.

Thinkowitz had his back to me and the approaching stranger as he spoke to Uco Azul.

I made my own approach.

"Greetings! Are you, Juani Negra? I'd like to..." and he dropped fearsome object glinting black in the midday sun, turned, and was off back over the hill.

I shouted over my shoulder to my partner that I had this and gave fierce chase up the hill.

From the grass and trees, I tasted that cherished flavor and my lungs pumped with fresh natural air.

Down the hill and into the next field.

Zig zagging through the seasonal installation of various types of door frames and archways to the god Janus, I closed in on him.

As he went around a marble archway, I leaped and clamped my hands on the lintel and with one pump and swing I shot myself boots-first onto Juani Negra.

He went down hard and I landed with knees on his back snapping out, "Assistant Sacred Detective Edwina Casaubon halting your progress for questioning."

"Sacred? Sacred? Not Profane? Fine. Yes. I'm complying. I'm sorry. I'm sorry I ran," he said.

I eased off of him and drew him to his feet by his arm.

We both caught our breath.

"Why did you think I'm Profane? Didn't you see my partner, Sacred Detective Rabbi Jakob Rabbinowitz?"

"Thinkowitz is here? Really? We've met in passing. I have a sincere respect for him. I didn't see him. I saw you. I've never seen you before, but you looked like City Safety Profane. And Sacredly, I'm clean. Not so for Profane. And that guilt took over. The guilt, I'm sorry."

"Guilt over what?" I asked.

"I, um, used some unallotted maguey from the neighborhood community garden," he said sheepishly.

"Was it for ritual purposes or to enhance your freak for a midday mind-away. Either way, why run? The penalty for using communal produce is extra personal effort to regrow or replace what was taken with personal home-cultivated crop."

"I know. I felt bad, so impulsive. Uco was coming over and midday mind-away is such a great Profane pleasure, a bonding Profane intoxication. I felt like a child, and I was trying to impress my friend. Uco is so cool. My crime was child-like laziness, and then I ran like a very unlazy child...

"I apologize. Truly. Deeply. It was just a reflex. The maguey will be replaced today after my rituals. But I have such guilt in me."

"I understand that. I had the dream last night."

"Yeah? Me too. Maybe there was some Dome-quake and you know it's believed that it can trigger a shame-shadow."

We walked back toward where Thinkowitz was with Uco Azul.

"I've heard. And it was a rough day for me also. So yesterday you were drinking pulque midday with Uco Azul."

"Yes, the situation I told you."

"Well, that's actually the reason we're here, to find out where you were then. The Oracle of Delphi has been murdered."

"Damn, Tiresias Pythia?! That is nuts-balls-bonkers. People are going to be upset. How'd it happen?"

"We don't have much to go on. But they were killed with an obsidian. We thought that might have meaning."

"But there's that obsidian on their altar. Everyone knows that. Is that what was used?" he asked, and I nodded. "Like everyone knows it's just the cyborg enhancements that make Tiresias—excuse me—made Tiresias such a good psychic, prophet, oracle. But some people didn't like to admit it."

"So, you don't think someone would do something like this to endorse Tiresias' power? To promote the idea that they was killed as confirmation of their veracity in order to encourage belief in Apollo specifically or the Greco-Hellenic Olympic pantheon in general."

"I don't think that would work. If anything, it does that for the SunSpot Cyborg Program."

Right then I thought about how strange it would be for my first case at Sacred to turn out to be Profane.

On the way down the hill to "Rock Garden - F" we picked up what I now know to be a macuahuitl.

"How was your exercise, Casaubon?" asked my partner as we arrived.

"I am deeply sorry my Profane guilt got a hold over me, Detective Rabbi. I have apologized to your partner and ask your forgiveness as well. I have nothing but respect for you," said Negra and turning to me: "and your partner too."

"All is forgiven, personally and officially. Uco Azul has confirmed your alibi for me and the Community Garden source of your Profane guilt," said Thinkowitz.

"He also had the dream last night," I added.

"Ah yes, the feelings it can trigger are quite deep. I sensed that maybe you too, Casaubon, had a similar night of sleep." He smiled calmingly at all three of us.

"Now, Juani Negra, I am sure my partner explained why we are here, but if you would be so kind as to join your friend in helping us expand our understanding of obsidian and its Sacred usage."

"Yeah, yes, as I was saying, and you can totally back me up on this, Juani. And we are so, like so happy to help. In the service of my god, Tezcatlipoca, and I think it's like not dissimilar for Jauni with Tohil, right?"

"Yes, by Tohil, I am in your service. We are the only devotees we know who have an active Sacred practice with obsidian. My god, Tohil, his name means 'obsidian' and blades made from it are used in bloodletting for sacrifice. Tohil likes blood, likes sacrifice, but it is that sacrifice that helps everyone," said Negra.

"And where do you get the blood," I asked.

"It is a sacrifice that the high priest makes," said Negra and popped-off his loose hooded-tunic. Standing in the high sun, refracted by the Dome into millions of broken beams of light, Juani Negra was enveloped in a jagged corona. His torso was a little older and looser than Azul's, but in this light, I found it even more stimulating.

With left arm outstretched, Negra raked his right fingers down the scar stripes on his left side. Then he switched hands and did the other side.

"Sometimes I also use beet juice," he said as if just to give me something to laugh at and break my gaze.

"Yeah, yes, and my god, Tezcatlipoca, yeah, his connection to obsidian is real important, like profound! But less on the blood and more on the visions that can rise from the smoking mirror that is obsidian. You know," added Uco Azul.

"And I would guess, I mean I don't know, but I would guess that it was a connection to the smoking mirror that was the reason that Tiresias had an obsidian on their altar," said Negra.

"So, Uco and Juani, would you both say that the obsidian possessed by the Oracle of Delphi was a widely known detail of their altar?" asked my partner.

Uco Azul made a naturally forced-looking thinking expression.

"I feel like I've always known, but I'm not sure how. People talk a lot about the Oracle of Delphi. Their predictions are pretty legendary. Esteemed. Probably from like just hanging out, people talking. 'You worship an obsidian god, did you know the Oracle has an obsidian on their altar,' that kind of thing. There aren't a lot of obsidian gods. I guess that is why you're here," said Negra.

"Yeah, there used to be that island with the heads, the ones with the big ears, and they had like man and woman gods that made obsidian," interjected Azul.

"Totally. Rapa Nui. There was a male obsidian god, Agekai, and a female, uh..." continued Negra searching for a word aloud.

"Hepeue," finished Thinkowitz.

"Yes! Exactly, but I don't know of anyone who worships them. We are your obsidian guys, but as we said, we didn't do this. Couldn't, and certainly wouldn't," said Negra.

"Uhm, like I don't mean to be weird, but how was an obsidian used on the Oracle?" asked Azul.

"It was placed with great force into the throat of Tiresias blocking the air-passage of their windpipe," replied my partner.

"Oh, well that, yeah, certainly doesn't sound like a sacrificial use of obsidian," said Negra. "For my tradition, and Uco's, it is important that you detectives understand that obsidian was seen as a type of blood originating from the earth. I don't know what Apollo would make of it, but from my view they choked on the blood of the earth. There is a terrible beauty to that death, but not Sacred in my tradition," said Negra.

"I believe our official business is concluded. Thank you, Uco Azul and Juani Negra, for your time and insight. Let us delay your rituals no longer," said Thinkowitz to their good byes and a round of smiles and bows.

We walked beyond the boundary of "Rock Garden - F" and at the edge of the park we stopped.

"Detective Rabbinowitz, you knew all of that already, all that they said about their gods and obsidian and other obsidian gods, right?"

"Yes, Casaubon, but I need to hear what they know and in what manner they know it. I do believe they had nothing to do with it, and the obsidian is a symbolic coincidence, but now there is less that we know that we don't know. Facts and knowledge matter less that what people do with them and how they relate to them."

I looked back at the men with their leopard spots and scar stripes. I was strangely ravenous.

WHERE ARE WE NOW?

My tempeh bánh mí was as exhilarating to my senses as the aerial dance performance overhead.

We sat in Decatur Square, a low area for community functions and dining surrounded by the usual Dome-reaching towers and pylons. After each bite I craned my neck.

A net was strung between two pylons that bordered the north and south corners of the square. Above it, in a colorful chaos of confounding choreography trapeze-swingers and silk-twirlers. Pole-dancers wind and invert around hanging brass poles.

The crunch of the toasted baguette; the spicy, tangy marinade on the tempeh; the cilantro leaf; the fresh slices of cucumber and jalapeño; the pickled carrot and daikon; the splash of lime juice; and the creamy burn of the chili nayonaisse. Every part of my palate was instigated and inflamed. Tongue, gums, and nose.

I was transported to times and places long gone, but people and cultures live on, all of them, under this Dome.

Directly above my head I recognized Primavera Yemi Paschal, who worshiped Osun and lived in my building. She rolled up and down within a sensuous pink silk, the dark creaminess of her skin refracting light in every direction. Soon I should observe my vow to speak with her, beyond passing pleasantries.

On my cheeks, brow, and in my hair, the whooshes tickled as the performers swung by. The slow languid pulses of their music reverberated in my ears and the tips of my fingers, sticky with nayonaisse.

Thinkowitz was taking in the same experience and our hands awkwardly brushed as we both reached for a skewer.

We shared an appetizer of speared barbacoa gluten and the texture, which ripped and tore so tenderly, radiated in my canine teeth. Our world is graced by so many fine chefs who have combined genetically modified botany, techno-emotional cooking, and all aspects of sluttiness into every possible culinary experience ever recorded in human history.

Our cuisine and entertainment are as pluralistic and polymorphous as our belief systems.

The awkward brush was a good instigator to break our comfortable silence.

"Negra mentioned Rapa Nui. Even though the people and land are gone, it is nice that the gods live on."

"A civilization is destroyed only when its gods are destroyed," Thinkowitz answered.

"Is that Maimonides?"

"No, a dark 20th philosopher who yearned for re-enchantment. A different early 20th century philosopher said modernity was a time of disenchantment. At the same time some already dreamed of re-enchantment. That, as you know, is what our RESURGA was all about. Re-enchantment, safety in cooperation, and freedom."

He bit into his flatbread, chewed, and continued.

"For the ancients, freedom meant the ability to switch gods, choice, true choice. The earliest of my people were henotheists as we all are now. We chose our god and it chose us right back. Monotheism wasn't just our foil because it merged with Kapital. Kapital was the final expression of the monotheistic urge, temptation, virus."

"I blame Akhenaten," I returned.

"And for this you would not be wrong," Thinkowitz replied. "Your people ran wild with the notion. The last pagan Roman poet, Rutilius Namatianus, once quipped, 'Would to the gods Judea had never been conquered.'"

"I will toast to that," I said and raised my mineral water. Thinkowitz continued as if he hadn't noticed, locked into his oration.

"Profane Prophet Walter Benjamin, a member of my tradition from the early 20th explained that Kapital developed as a parasite of christianity and overtook the host where christianity's history became a history of the parasite itself."

I returned to my bánh mí a little sullen now and left him the silence to fill if he needed. The guilt. The dream. Azul. Negra. The sustenance needed to right me. I looked up as I chewed. Cilantro, lime, chili, tempeh, jalapeño, baguette crunch... Primavera spinning in pink silk...

Thinkowitz returned to his flatbread.

I began to feel bold.

"Negra also said something else. After I brought him to the ground with a tactical tackle and ended his flight, we cleared up why he ran and then got around to the case and the fate of Tiresias Pythia. I asked him if he thought someone might have killed Tiresias to promote the Oracle's power. To proselytize for Apollo or Olympians. But he knew all about the cyborg-enhancements and off-handedly mentioned that endorsing the SunSpot Cyborg program would be a more realistic motive."

"Do you know why people commit Sacred crimes like homicide, Casaubon?" He was being rhetorical and left no space for me to answer. "The possibility of true spiritual power or divinity motivates believers to Sacred crimes."

"There might be some credence to Negra's theory and it is a stone we will not leave unturned. However I have received messages from the Brothers Panic, and a few other contacts, that there is already much chatter and buzz spreading rapidly through our inter-connected environment, beyond the adherents of a Greek-mythos, about the Oracle's dangerous power. There is awe, there is fear, and there is desire stoked all around us. People might know all about the cyborg-enhancements, as Negra does, but the desire to believe in something bigger than us is just so strong that many find it very easy to over-look facts and evidential truths," he concluded.

"So, you don't think there is the possibility that this investigation is Profane after all?" I asked.

"What we do bridges Sacred and Profane. You can't have one without the other. I understand you come from Profane, Casaubon, and there is a necessary distinction in our work between these two types of crimes. What we do is fundamentally Sacred. We engage mystery. And this will seem to go against the whole point of our vocation, but we never actually solve a mystery. We solve crimes, something inherently Profane. And we will find out who killed Tiresias. That is a commitment I have made to my god, this City, and so many others. However, there will still be mystery. We uncover spots of ground so we can walk through the darkness with a sure foot.

"The Oracle of Delphi is dead. They were very effective in that role due to cyborg-enhancements, but maybe something else was also there? The loss of a beloved spiritual presence, embraced by the devotees of several different gods, is the domain of Sacred. But alas, the motive of the killer might be Profane. We shall find out," said Thinkowitz.

The aerial performance concluded as sky-born youth, worshippers of various winged-deities, who have been running up and down these pylons since they could walk parachuted and jacket-glided down through the trapeze-swingers and silk-twirlers and thudded a chorus of giggles down around us on the net.

Her Hundred Miles to Hell

On his way out of the City Safety Sacred Homicide office, late in the day on my first Friday and second day, Thinkowitz—who had been silent for hours—stopped me in the middle of my paperwork.

"Casaubon, I am quite happy to be your partner and mentor you in the ways of Sacred investigation. I find you pleasant to be around and after reading your record I was a part of the decision to promote you and take you on as a partner.

"However, there is another reason why you have been assigned to me, or moreover, why I might need a partner. As you might already be aware, I respect the Sabbath of my people. There is somewhere our investigation can only take us on a Saturday, but alas, I cannot work."

"So, I am to go alone?" I asked.

"I will be there with you, but only as an observer. You will do all of the official engagement. I will not speak on work matters, but I can brief you ahead of time on mythic context, for that is just the sharing of information," he paused. It was after sunset and he was out of our work pod, ready to walk down the long flight of stairs before his long walk home.

"We are going back to the Temple of Delphi. This time to visit the bottom floors, Tartarus, to speak to the undertaker there about whether he noticed anything out of the ordinary yesterday in the morning. Tomorrow, in the Roman-mythos is the day of Saturn, but for the Greek-mythos it is the day of Cronos, interpretable as his syncretic twin. It is the one day of the week that Tartarus is open for business. The one day I cannot conduct business."

The next morning, I exited the tram at the 10th Street stop and Thinkowitz was waiting for me. I knew he had walked there, but he didn't look tired. Just a pensive face broken momentarily by the serene smile of welcome.

We walked up half the block and then heading down the other side we were struck by an unexpected sight.

Throngs of people, clumped and crowded, around the base of the structure. Much black for mourning, and a colorful array of touched-up clothing and elaborate costumes in tribute and veneration. Wreaths and draperies of laurel. Black dolphins. A walking Doric column.

They were drawn to the power of this place, newly charged. I felt it two days past. I'm not even a believer. Evidence is the greatest threat to disbelief. For some.

Passing through the crowd, and past the uniformed City Safety Officer, we ascended the flight of stone steps and at the top looked down at them. This was love. This was devotion. This was belief.

We entered the dim reception area of Tartarus on what was technically the second floor. Something was waiting for us. I could feel expectancy.

Standing just within the threshold was a dark shadowy form. On first apprehension it seemed inanimate, but statuesque would be an understatement.

The posture of this form warmed and softened as my partner spoke.

"Hello, N'Deye Frimbo, my visit today is social, for it is the Sabbath. I bear you the deepest of condolences on the loss of your friend and neighbor. May their god bless them, and may Tartarus bless you."

Tartarus is not only a place, but according to Hesiod, the third entity that came into being, after Chaos and Earth— Gaia—and before Eros, Love, conveyed Thinkowitz on our way.

Frimbo emerged from the shadows, producing and lighting a candle. I put him at seven inches over six feet and his skin rivaled the shadows in darkness. Easily five shades darker than my own. It was a lovely shimmering darkness.

He held the candle out to my partner and together they shared in bearing the light. There was a slight bow between them and then Frimbo turned to me.

"Detective?"

"Respectful greetings, I'm Assistant Sacred Detective Edwina Casaubon. I am here to ask you some questions, but allow me first to extend my condolences for the loss of your friend and neighbor."

He offered me the same slight bow and returned to silent, rigid standing.

In the hanging silence, I allowed myself the distraction of looking around. The darkness was opening up to through the candle's faint efforts. It was a clean room, stylistically simple, and appropriate for greeting the aggrieved. This was just one floor. Where was the place that is also a god?

Thinkowitz stood quietly behind me, but his presence felt different. In all of our interactions over the last two days I felt him mentoring in his observation of my movements. Today he was just there. Present.

"See it, Detective? Would you like to? Before your questions. See it?" N'Deye Frimbo asked. Now someone else was observing and reading me.

I nodded and we followed him to a wide double door at the back of the room. He opened them and we all entered.

Down one level in a wide lift, one that must accommodate supine bodies.

The doors opened and just beyond the shaky threshold was a darkness that seemed to resist light, to banish light. The light stayed with us in the lift, falling behind and upward. Before me was a void with presence. My stomach dropped within me.

With a subtle gesture-command, Frimbo turned on even-positioned wall sconces all around the room and the darkness was cast back and down. A hole was set into the floor, it's blackness complete, appearing like a twenty-foot-wide slice of obsidian nestled into concrete.

No railing, border, or boundary, before us was a funereal pit at a point of purity and perfection. City inspected and sanctioned. Mythically sanctified and Sacralized.

Is this where Tiresias Pythia will face eternity?

The words of Thinkowitz reverberated in my head:

Tartarus is a place of punishment for gods or those who affront the gods.

Hesiod tells us Tartarus is as far below the earth as the heavens are above, an anvil will fall nine days before it reaches the bottom.

"Surely, it's not that deep," I let slip out loud.

"Pardon?" asked Frimbo.

"Is this Tartarus as deep as Hesiod once described?" I asked.

The tall figure bent at the waist all the way over and lifted a brick of marble from a perfect stack by the wall and tossed it without a glance over his shoulder into the pit.

"Return in eight and a half days. Listen. And wait," he said and walked past me back into the lift and waited next to Thinkowitz.

As the lift drew us back upwards, Frimbo explained to me that there was another room on the second floor in which the bodies are kept and preparations for rituals are enacted.

We returned to the reception room and I continued with the official investigation as we all stood. Frimbo never offered seating or comfort, but his rigidity, like that of the room, was not one of coldness.

"Did you see or hear anything strange or different the morning of Thursday, two days hence?" I asked.

"Thursday morning. There was some trouble. I didn't report it. It was nothing I couldn't handle. They understood that. That is why they left."

"They?" I asked.

"Members of a nihilist cult."

"Abyssoids, yes?" confirmed Thinkowitz.

"How is a cult allowed? City statutes are pretty clear that groupings of shared worship or veneration of the same deific object are frowned upon," I said looking to my partner.

"They're nihilists, Casaubon. Technically they believe in nothing, so it skirts the letter of our City suggestion. I've kept my eye on them. I've wanted to debate them, but that has yet to come to pass," he clarified to us both and ended with an aside to me.

"Can we go to speak to them after sundown?"

"Now you are thinking like my partner, Casaubon."

Defecating Ecstasy

After sunset we reconvened at a centrally located tram stop in Midtown.

I had spent the afternoon back at City Safety while Thinkowitz wandered Midtown in quiet penitent reflection on his god and faith, as he explained. Now he was back on the job and we headed west on the elevated tram to Bolton.

Coming down the pylon lift at the Bolton stop, I could see the cultivated green space of Highway 285, a belt of mostly-raised field and forest that wraps around City proper separating out the suburbs.

For all the anxiety a Domed-existence can induce, for all of the guilt deep in my being and the Dome-quake dreams that can stir it, seeing our various belts and bands of green, cutting through such a thickness of towers and pylons, my hope feels a little less sullen.

From the tram pylon we walked up Bolton to the crumbling shell of a building hundreds of years old. Our records show that it had missed development by no meaningful reason of its own. A relic of the 20th through which once passed destructive and inefficient conveyances not unlike our trams. Now it is an artefact amongst the art of our towering buildings and pylons.

As we entered the within the broken building, onto a dusty concrete floor, we heard voices.

Booming down from above the voices were chanting, a rhythmic, repetitive cycle of words in call and response.

Dirt is the dominant

Dirt is the dominant

Dirt always wins

Dirt always wins

Dirt fills the void

We fill the dirt

We fill the dirt

I followed my partner as he followed the voices up a rickety flight of metal stairs. He seemed nervous, maybe even a little fearful, but he pushed on undaunted.

On the second floor of girders and grating, we found the source of the voices. Four people in matte black jumpsuits congregating against the remaining corner of a brick wall.

"Greetings! This is City Safety, Sacred Homicide division, Detectives Rabbi Jakob Rabbinowitz and Edwina Casaubon," Thinkowitz called out to them.

The chanting stopped, and the black-clad forms, sheltered from the City and the night by a brittle brick wall turned slowly towards us.

"Hello, Detectives," came from at least one of them as we moved in closer.

They greeted us with a cool aloofness and gave us their names. Two women: Violet Burt and Crenshaw Maccabee. And two men: Tungsten Kung and Lucite Berenger.

While getting introductions, I was looking around, assessing, as I knew my partner was also. If he was looking for what wasn't here that would be a long negative list. The second floor where they were congregating was as empty of everything but dust and rubble as the rest of the building.

"We beg your forgiveness for disturbing your ritual," said my partner.

"We're just chanting. Pure vocal hedonism. No meaning to it," said Violet Burt.

"Just like everything," said Lucite Berenger.

"If you say so. We are here to ask you a few questions in regard to...," began Thinkowitz, somewhat flummoxed before he was interrupted.

"The death of the Oracle of Delphi?" asked Tungsten Kung.

"The death of the priestess of Apollo?" asked Crenshaw Maccabee, mockingly.

"The death of the cyborg oracle," said Lucite Berenger, his mocking tone laced with derision.

"I have gathered that you are not believers," said Thinkowitz.

"I believe that cyborgs exist," said Lucite Berenger, glaring steel-gray eyes at my partner.

"But, you worship nothing?" asked Thinkowitz.

"Why not? Nothing last forever," answered Violet Burt.

"And nothing is better than sex," added Lucite Berenger.

"Why do you bother N'Deye Frimbo, the Undertaker at Tartarus?" asked Thinkowitz.

"We want to get into his hole," said Crenshaw Maccabee. She was at the back of the clump of the black-clad beings. Their heads were all shaved short and the hair dyed black. The posture of the group fluctuated between sullen and ironically sullen with random punctuations of mirth and anger.

"We are enthralled by his void," said Violet Burt.

"Let me guess, what makes the largest hole in the City so great? Nothing?" cut in Thinkowitz.

"Cheers, Sacred Detective Rabbi Jakob Rabbinowitz, you have us figured out," said Tungsten Kung.

"Just look at Thinkowitz thinking about and finally understanding nothing," smirked Lucite Berenger.

I felt a beat, a moment of charged silence, hang there between us all and I had no idea of what might happen next. From what I understood about my partner, the Abyssoids represented and expressed his very antithesis. He valued humility and scorned arrogance. He respected sincere belief and learning.

"Thursday morning around 11:30, someone violently shoved a fist-sized disc of obsidian into the mouth of Tiresias Pythia, breaking their teeth and obstructing air-flow to the lungs. The Oracle of Delphi died an agonizing death before the eyes of the perpetrator," he said with authority and the moment was gone, like it had never been.

"The perpetrator had an appointment to hear the Oracle's prophecy. So, you all who do not worship Apollo or any of the Olympian gods of the Greco-mythic system and believe in nothing most likely do not include a perpetrator of this Sacred crime.

"My second question is whether you saw anything that morning that might be out of the ordinary or useful in our investigation," asked Thinkowitz.

"We went up the stairs and banged on the door to Tartarus. The giant drove us back down the stairs," said Lucite Berenger.

"It was early. There was nothing out of the ordinary," said Tungsten Kung.

"Unlike today..." said Crenshaw Maccabee.

"Today?" asked Thinkowitz.

"We didn't get too close. We couldn't," said Crenshaw Maccabee.

"So many fools missing the giant's big nothing for the fake power of the cyborg oracle and their silly golden god," said Lucite Berenger.

"We went to see the spectacle, Detective. Just before coming here. It's all everyone is talking about. A surge of new belief," said Crenshaw Maccabee.

"Fools and misdirected belief," said Lucite Berenger. "The oracle's only power was cyborg power. Sun-power. Real power. That is worth killing for. The same power that makes trees green. Fools. They know it, but they don't want to," said Lucite Berenger.

"And you are the unfoolish four? Those blessed by nothing to believe in nothing?" asked Thinkowitz.

"Maybe not believing in anything, or believing in nothing, is just our way of fighting that affliction we suffer from, you know virus B-23," said Violet Burt.

"What is that?" I ask.

"You know, Unease Disease... Disquietude Syndrome... you have it. We all do," added Crenshaw Maccabee.

"Virus B-23, is that from Burroughs or Maawaam?" Thinkowitz asked.

"That certainly doesn't matter," said Lucite Berenger

"But nothing does, Lucite," said Tungsten Kung.

"And that's what's great about nothing. It matters," Violet Burt.

"We are Voidoids!" said all of the black forms in an obviously dissonant missed harmony.

"I thought you were called Abyssoids," I puzzled at them.

"Names don't matter," said Crenshaw Maccabee.

"Nothing matters," said Lucite Berenger.

"And that's why we worship it," said a few of the voices at once with a sound of zeal that bordered on the ridiculous.

It was clear there was nowhere further we could go. So clear my partner and I reached the same conclusion silently. We thanked them, said goodbye, and gave slight bows. As we downed the stairs a ghastly and stupid cacophony of chanting about dirt followed.

"So, did you get the debate you were hoping for?" I asked my partner as we left the building.

"I don't think they are sincere but maybe the levels of irony are so deep they have accidentally found depth. Their whole theology is pun-based. How can I argue with that? They should worship Proteus, his shifting form might provide amusement and inspiration...

"And yet, humor aside, I do feel for them and worry about them on a psychological level. Maimonides tells us, 'when a person considers himself to be wicked, he will not hesitate to transgress. There will be no sin that he will consider too severe to transgress.' It is not healthy to think one is nothing. Even our sullen hope is still hope," he said sweetly and sincerely.

"Lucite Berenger did say something familiar," I added.

"I know what you are thinking, Casaubon. That is the second mention of the same potentially Profane motive."

"Who would stand to benefit if the SunSpot Cyborg Program became more popular? Certainly, no motive could be greed, who could physically handle that?" I asked.

"Of course, there is no potential profit for anyone. The SunSpot Cyborg Program is a totally public entity controlled by the citizens of the City for the good of the City. The City Sovereign is on the Board of Directors for the Program. If anyone could benefit, he could. No stone unturned, Casaubon. Tomorrow we go to see the Sovereign!"

Then Jump In the River Holding Hands

Our church is the front room of our family home in Roswell.

Our household god, the father of our christ, the anointed one, we worship together as a family on Sunday mornings.

We hold hands. We say our prayer. My parents make a simple meal. No cross, no props, one bible.

I stayed even less time than normal. I didn't want to speak to them about the investigation until I knew something real, something true.

We weren't going to City Hall, but to the Sovereign's residence and home office, so I met my partner,

Sacred Detective Rabbi Jakob Rabbinowitz at the Peachtree Tower tram stop.

This part of downtown was a place of well-maintained relics, building technology that feels more ancient than just over a couple hundred years. Not much really changed until there was no choice.

I looked up at the staid design of Peachtree Tower. Orderly, dignified, beige stones standing one on top of another around windows of the same long, standing rectangle shapes.

Seven hundred and seventy feet high, before the Dome supports, and topped with two columned enclosures reservable for rituals and rites, Peachtree Tower provided living quarters for many and we honored the Sovereign with the top.

We took the lift to the fifty-second floor which had tall, arched windows I always dreamed of viewing the City through, and entered into an austere foyer with a style thrown back to the early days of the RESURGA, with obvious touch-walls less-integrated into a greater concept and rooms divided by touch-glass partitions.

This was the home of Ped Malus, our City Sovereign, and his wife, Spendeva Luna. He worshipped the Roman goddess of justice and civic duty, Justitia. She worshipped Ceres, a Roman goddess of agriculture, fertility, and maternal relations.

He was about sixty, no one was entirely sure. Like many of his generation he was raised entirely by the City. A true product of this world. She was seventy-five and they have only been married ten years now. Once he was appointed Sovereign, he allowed himself the rewards of comfort and domesticity.

Ped Malus was an easy choice for the appointment. Born during the last years of Dome completion. It was a rough time. He was orphaned or abandoned.

But young Ped Malus, named by City care workers for his clubbed left foot, had a mind for puzzles. He apprenticed with City engineers from an early age. Justitia, he worshipped from a double sense of devotion.

Ultimately, he was instrumental in resolving the final issue with Dome-leak. In this way he saved us all. But his Dome-work raced against time. Many died before his eyes. From there he worked with a team to develop the SunSpot Cyborg Program. This is why he didn't marry until late. He was working in gratitude and repentance both.

I had never met them, but everyone knew them. There was no doubt who he was when he entered and greeted us with a kind, but stiff formality. He still walked with a slight limp.

She entered just a moment after him and stood at his side, placing her hand in his, fingers trying and failing for a moment to interlock.

There was a nervousness to their fidget. Suspicious. Guilty?

They saw me notice and apologized for not being better hosts, they both had the dream last night.

I felt for them. I was lucky. If there was any Dome-quake, I felt nothing.

Two of our most beautiful and best citizens stood before me. She had a lithe, shimmering-elegance and long silvery hair against skin far lighter than my own. It was the lightest skin I'd ever seen—a pink peachiness—and yet still pleasing. She wore a day gown of gray mesh and nothing else. His simple gray robe complimented her. He wasn't much to describe— a man with skin and hair as brown as my own—but his beauty was in his dignity and devotion. It was the job of my partner and myself to question them.

Thinkowitz took the lead, as his position and rapport with the Sovereign dictated.

After formalities, he asked each where they were Thursday morning and they both were here. They were each other's alibi, but that is not strange for a couple in their home.

"Is this about Tiresias Pythia, the Oracle of Delphi?" asked the Sovereign.

"Oh dear! So tragic. A true tragedy," said Spendeva Luna.

"From both an official and personal stance, I extend deep gratitude at that you are on this investigation, Detective Rabbi. And you, Detective Casaubon, are very fortunate to have this learning experience, you are in capable hands. And I know that the legacy and memory of the Oracle of Delphi will be honored and served justice. What can we do to help, and why do you need to know where we were Thursday?" asked the Sovereign.

We entered behind them farther into the wide foyer and sat on stiff chairs before the settee on which the couple positioned themselves.

"Dear Sovereign, we believe that establishing motive is integral in understanding what happened and who the killer is. One potential motive involves the SunSpot Cyborg Program. It is likely Tiresias Pythia was murdered because of their power and if people understand where that power really comes from it would be a boon for the Program. Promoting the program could be a motive," explained Thinkowitz.

"Ah, yes," said the Sovereign. "I understand."

He rose from the settee and went to the nearest arched window. Spendeva Luna remained seated with a polite smile, in a position of attention.

"Do you see that down there?" he asked, pointing across and down at the circular, black glass exterior of the Peachtree Plaza, almost as high as where we were.

Several of those floors housed the offices and some of the laboratories of the SunSpot Cyborg Program.

"It should be familiar to you, Detective Rabbi Jakob Rabbinowitz, and even to you, Detective Casaubon. It is familiar to everyone, because it belongs to everyone. I serve on the Board of Directors for the SunSpot Cyborg Program. I am not a leader of the Program, but serve as moderator, for we are a Board of all equals, sharing in responsibility and blame. This Program is public and belongs to the City, as do I as Sovereign. The City and the Program both exist to serve each of you as well as every other citizen.

"It took great sacrifice to get here, the sacrifice of individuals, and the sacrifice of families, and we must honor them, we must honor those families who have lost so much, lost so much they can never get back. This City has given me everything, has made me who I am. Stopping the Dome-leak from the terrible power of the sun began the shared effort of devising ways to capture that terrible power. We have harnessed an unstoppable force and direct it into the highest quality of life the world has ever seen.

"Like the psalm in your tradition, Detective Rabbi, the lovely one you taught me about a 'cup that runs over,' once everyone was fed and physical care easy to maintain, we directed that overflow of energy and power into expanding human potential. Some lives saved, some enhanced.

"I, we, want to honor those families and their sacrifices. Tiresias' death is no boon for the Program, but a loss. There is nothing to gain. They was one of our greatest achievements. As are you, Detective Rabbi," he concluded.

Spendeva Luna rose from the settee with a grace I admired and stood at her husband's side. She placed a hand on his shoulder, as if in comfort and they both looked out the window together down at the Peachtree Plaza.

Thinkowitz rose and I followed. He conveyed our gratitude to the Sovereign and his wife for their time and drawn from their moment at the window they returned thanks and wished us a quick resolution to this investigation.

THE SERIOUS MOONLIGHT

The electric Moon throbbed full and low over the dance floor.

Revelers, worshippers spun and shook and flailed in ecstasy and inebriation while the Moon rotated and cycled through all its phases.

Waxing.

Waning.

Dark side.

Sea of Tranquility.

It was Monday evening and we had met at the Fabulous Fox Theater at the bottom of Midtown.

Thinkowitz's sources notified him about a Moon Deity Pantheon Party scheduled in the historic theater now used for rituals, performances, and even parties. It was here he hoped to gain insight into a surge in Greco-mythic worship possibly inspired by the death of the Oracle of Delphi.

We stood along the northern wall and watched as twelve dancers, half in flowy robes of touched-up sheets and half in touch-cloth skin-suits all touch-set to mirror, entered the dance floor from opposing points and with perfect choreography rotated with the cycles of the holographic Moon overhead. Their costumes at once reflected and embodied the celestial orb above.

This low building was preserved during the RESURGA, along with its gross display of 20th orientalism, but repurposed like everything else in our world for everyone to share. What was once a parody of otherness has been embraced with sincerity and this mixture of medieval Moorish and ancient Egyptian design is the perfect place for Moon worship.

It is easy to feel a form of microcosmic meta-vertigo, as the dance floor and stage—serving tonight as a mingle floor—are designed to feel like an Arabian courtyard, outside and under an evening sky of ninety-six crystal stars. Tonight, the Moon is low under that sky and over the courtyard dance floor. All within this medieval mosque shell with its own Domed top.

Watching the Moon turn and the spinning of the dancers below it, I felt a deep charge and throb and then relaxation in my uterus, like a sigh, as the last of my blood had only dripped away this morning. The New Moon began last Thursday, January sixth, the day of Tiresias' death, and I knew I was not alone here with this feeling. Most everyone around me must have felt their final drips of shedding today or yesterday or will tomorrow.

From dark to light the Moon shed its skin above the dance floor, over and over again, as dancers like Moon-drops spun into and away from each other. I felt an understand of their attraction, but wanted to know more.

"Why today? Why this Monday?" I asked my partner.

"The schedule for these Pantheon Parties is always the first Monday after the New Moon. This allows for the next Monday, or Moon-day, to be free for personal worship before the Full Moon, which will be on the twentieth of January. One, twenty, twenty-two twenty will have a nice ring to it for numerologist for the Full Moon this month and year.

"My tradition is not dissimilar in its adherence to this monthly lunar calendar. We start our month with the first light after the New Moon, which was last Friday, or last Thursday after sunset," said Thinkowitz.

For a moment, taken by my surroundings, I became very excited for the egg I will ovulate on one, twenty, twenty-two twenty, before Thinkowitz pulled me out of my reverie.

"Come, Casaubon, let us encounter some avatars. You seemed to be enchanted by Astrape and Bronte, that level of devotion," said Thinkowitz, and I followed him to the bar at the side of the dance floor.

He was correct. I have never felt a closeness to my god as so many of the adherents I have encountered since my promotion to Sacred and moving into the center of the City do to their own. Especially, the avatars. An inseparable closeness of mystical or constant shamanic oneness baffled me.

Passing across the dance floor I recognized one of the twelve dancers taking a break.

Summer Dahlia lived in my new building. We had spoken a few times in passing at the lift and tram stop. I knew she worshipped the Hawai'ian moon goddess, Lona, but now I got to behold her in such wonderfully choreographed veneration. It was lovely how her body moved in a touch-up skin-suit of mirrors. She looked one with the electric moon she reflected. Soon she will have her birth-penis surgically transformed and menstruation will be possible. Regardless of menstruation, she epitomized womanhood in a way that inspired me.

At the bar on the south side of the dance floor Thinkowitz introduced me to Luna, Diana, and Hubal. Diana was a man who worshipped in full-commitment as avatar to the goddess. He wore a light, sheer tunic belted with a stag head buckle, a golden cloak, and purple half-boots. He was Diana. He was the goddess and he was a man. His long brown hair was tied back in a loose ponytail. This goddess was showing Luna his golden arrows.

Luna also wore a light, sheer tunic, but tied with a golden chord. Her long blonde hair was braided up on her head around a golden crescent crown. She held the golden arrows in a way that Hubal could also see from his angle at the bar.

Hubal wore a thick, white robe, his whole modest outfit bereft of detail or ornament except for a solid metallic right hand of a golden color.

Diana, Luna, and Hubal, respectively Roman, Roman, and Arabian moon deities, were polite, but intense. The strangest thing was the banal chitchat they made with Thinkowitz while still presenting as gods. None of them had visited the Oracle, but they mourned Tiresias Pythia and directed us to their friend, a worshipper of Artemis, further down the bar.

"Casaubon, this is Alli Verbena. She has been an Olympian devotee her whole life and was very close with Tiresias Pythia," said Thinkowitz.

"I'm sorry for your loss," I started to say, but she embraced me before I could finish and held me close.

Her sweat felt nice and mixed with what rose out of me from the heat and energy of this place. She smelled of the potently inebriating nectar cocktail that was being served.

Before she pulled away there was a moment where it felt like she had let go and all her weight was on me and in my arms. In that moment I didn't want her to let go.

Drawn back, I saw that she was dressed in a similar tunic to both Diana and Luna. It clung to her moist body and her long brown hair stuck to her forehead, neck, and shoulders.

We were properly introduced and Thinkowitz asked her about new converts to the Greco-mythos. She confirmed the rise. That to not be outdone, people were even digging up naiads and dryads to worship.

"I only know one new convert to Olympians or the Greco-mythos who is here tonight. Her name is Kiki Selavy. I know she used to worship an Etruscan moon goddess, Artume, and would come to these parties repping that goddess, but she's here tonight all about Hecate. We had a drink earlier. She seems darker, maybe," said Alli Verbena. "But maybe it's because she never visited the Oracle.

We found Kiki Selavy by the north bar sipping a Negroni slushy not too different from the nectar cocktails most were having. While she wasn't one of the twelve dancers, she still wore a skin-suit but of touched-up geological swirls constantly moving. Pearl. Moonstone. Mica. Oil-spill. Constant swirls.

She was about the same height and darkness of complexion as I, but a slimmer build, most likely from yoga. Her skin-suit was hypnotic, but also fun, and she glistened with the same sheen of sweat as most revelers here.

"Oh, hi!" she greeted us, after we introduced ourselves. I deduced a human of depth and complexity hidden beneath chipperness. On each of her bare shoulders was a key in what looked like fresh inking.

"If you would be so kind, would you tell us how you came to the decision recently of transferring your devotion to Hecate in the Greco-mythos from an Etruscan deity?" asked Thinkowtiz over the music.

"Oh...," and her mood and tone darkened. "Well, Artume was great and all. She was of my family's tradition and gave me a connection to a distant ancient place and also the Moon. The Moon really governs me. I feel it in every way. My moods. My cycle. My power. I lead a yoga session at night. No Sun salutation. We salute the Moon..."

She drifted off with a thinking face of pursed lips and then came back.

"I had heard of the Oracle of Delphi for years. I have Greco-mythos friends—and even some Roman and Etruscan-mythos friends—who just rave and rave about them. Raved. I never went though. I think I was scared. I guess I thought they would see, somehow, the real me. The me I wasn't being. The me I was scared to be. The me I was scared to show my friends and family. And then they were gone. It's so horrible. Who could do that to someone? To someone so special? Someone so important to so many lives," she wept a little and then snorted it all back in and widening her eyes dry took a large sip from her drink.

"I know it's trite. I know there are dozens or maybe even hundreds of people out there trying to find their own connection to Olympus now. Chasing that source of truth and power. But I feel like I've been reborn with the death of the Oracle. They are not here to see me as I am, so I have faced myself. I honor their death. With this New Moon, I am new. I am devoted to Hecate, to *SHE WHO WORKS HER WILL*, the Goddess of Night and Cross-Roads and Sorcery. To entryways once locked and forbidden," and she crossed her arms and pointed with two fingers on each hand to the keys on each shoulder.

"Hecate was never welcomed on Olympus. Not lofty, she was out in the world of that Greco-mythos, leading women in opposition. Helping them cultivate their power, the power of the earth, the power of their bodies, the power of the Moon!" she said triumphantly, if not also a little drunkenly.

In the limited time that we encountered Kiki Selavy, I saw a range of her humanity and phases like the electric Moon hanging over the dance floor before me. Her power felt real and her devotion sincere. Tiresias Pythia was still changing lives from beyond this world. Selavy invited us to attend her Moon Salutation Yoga workshop that she gives most evenings in Piedmont Park. More confirmation, but no new information. At least I found an intriguing new yoga option.

As the night wound on, we moved through the crowds of mostly women on the fringes of the dance floor and across the stage. I encountered worshippers of Moon deities I had never heard of. Since our goal was to find those of the Greco-(or even Roman)-mythos, Thinkowitz whispered in my ear a constant commentary:

She worships Kuu, Moon goddess of Finnish tradition; she worships Hiuke, Norse god of the waxing Moon not to be confused with Bil, Norse god of waning Moon; she worships Yemoja, a Yoruba mother goddess associated with the Moon; she worships Alignak a lunar god of the Inuit...

He seemed to know everyone, just like he seemed to know everything.

Making contact with those who had visited the Oracle of Delphi, I collected testimonies with a wide prophetic territory, like:

The Oracle told me I lost my chapstick on the way to our session and when I left, I found it right there where they said, half a block away, said Meena Gar, a worshipper of

Selene, Greek Moon goddess daughter of the Sun and the Dawn.

The Oracle held my hand and softly, kindly told me I had cancer, that it was very early, and after I left, I went for a scan that was positive and we began treatment immediately, said Daisy Chao, a worshipper of Cynthia, an aspect of Artemis.

The Oracle told me I was in love with my best friend and the sooner I admitted that the easier life would flow, and they were right, and we are still together years later, said Honey Han, a worshipper of Phoebe, another aspect of Artemis.

The Oracle guided me over the years with my understanding of who I am and my destiny and when they told me I was living the wrong gender I knew they were correct, said Bea Sentinel, a worshipper of Bendis, a Thracian huntress goddess associated with the Moon.

The Oracle revealed that I was pregnant when I was only three weeks along and they knew it would be a boy. They told me to name him Elijah, the name of a prophet they respected outside both of our traditions, said Danielle LeFevers, a worshipper of Isis, an Egyptian goddess with lunar connections. LeFevers visited the Oracle of Delphi due to mythic connections and how strong the Oracle's reputation was for truth-telling.

After collecting all of this data, I too was finding it hard to question the power of blind Tiresias Pythia, the Oracle of Delphi, the prophet, the seer, the truth-teller.

I looked to my partner for sensibility and reason.

"We all each love our god and believe in our god and there is no denying the devotion Tiresias Pythia had for Apollo, Casaubon. But you know the Oracle's history, you know of the cyborg enhancements. With sight denied, every other sense has been amplified. They perceived the world with a clearer and wider reach than you or I could ever imagine. They absorbed distant sense data and had the ability to sort and connect it all.

"Almost every example of their power that you heard tonight could be explained through distant hearing and close listening, the smell of pheromones and hormones, complicated and obvious deduction based on that sense data. It's all there," he said.

"How about the woman whose pregnancy they deduced? There is no hormone or bodily indicator for the sex or gender of a child?" I challenged.

"The odds were with them with a one in three or four chance," he smiled and shrugged.

As we left, a robed dancer sat crying on the floor by the side door out onto Ponce de Leon Avenue. Copious tears fell onto her mirrored fabric, swirling and sliding down in a pearline shimmer. She covered her mouth, but frightful shrieks escaped her fingers. Rhythmically, and randomly. Piercingly. Up my spine. In my stomach.

I bent to ask her if she was alright.

My partner stopped me with a gentle hand and drew me back. He leaned in and whispered his commentary: *her name is Flinn Hill and she is a Lachrymology Therapist with a practice for assisting in grief. She worships Agusaya, Babylonian goddess of loud crying, and as an aspect of Ishtar there is a moon connection, hence her presence here.*

Regardless of her different mythic tradition, here she was channeling her own feelings of loss—as well as those of others—around Tiresias Pythia.

Out on the street, the music from the party was muted behind closed doors to the point of a dull presence, but I could still hear and feel her wailing shrieks. They were inside me. Cutting like a scythe. Like the silver blade of the Moon overhead.

Animal Grace

We were working side by side in our office pod when a message came in for me from an old friend in Profane.

Profane Safety Officer Meiko Ran had a tip. A goat was missing from the City Zoological Sanctuary. This unto itself is a severe crime, but a solidly Profane one—until motive or use of the goat can be established. Due to the confusing nature of the Oracle's death and the various theories grape-vining around the City, Meiko Ran thought it might be connected.

Tuesday had been a slow day so far in regard to information, leads, or tips, and I was taking this time to work on this record of my first assignment in Sacred. My first assignment learning all of the overlapping worlds of the City with the one person who understood it better than all others, my new partner, Sacred Detective Rabbi Jakob "Thinkowitz" Rabbinowitz.

No stone unturned, as Thinkowitz would often say.

So, we were off to the City Zoological Sanctuary downtown in Centennial Olympic Park. We took a tram from City Safety Headquarters directly to the south entrance of the Sanctuary at Marietta Street and met Meiko Ran there.

Meiko conveyed the details: Early this morning, when the Veterinary staff was checking on each Zoological specimen and preparing the various morning meals the goat enclosure tally was one short. The missing goat was a small Nubian female of caramel and burnt umber coloration named MacAvoy, called Mac by her caregivers.

There were several established points of entrance and egress around the whole Sanctuary with less free-range for the public on the north side around the aquatic enclosure.

We thanked Meiko and Thinkowitz told her that we would see her again at the goat enclosure, he wanted to walk the perimeter.

We walked in silence northeast up a path parallel to Centennial Olympic Park Drive. It was still early in the day and the Sanctuary has kept the public clear of the grounds in expectation of our arrival. We looked for disturbances or signs of break-in.

Thinkowitz was in his crime scene mode. Looking for what wasn't there. Looking for the negative presence.

I noticed the humming again. That same humming from when we moved about the inner sanctum of the Oracle of Delphi.

Maybe he was louder because he was more comfortable around me. Maybe I was getting attuned to my august partner's ways. But it was very clearly "Zoo Zoo Jupiter" being hummed.

Here it made sense; we were at a Zoological Sanctuary. At Delphi it did not, but the overlapping context is investigation, shallow thought, wide awareness.

The song was about a Zoo on the planet Jupiter with specimens from the whole solar system, even humans. The actuality of where we were was different from the message of this very old song. Here we might be containing animals, but unlike human/animal relations of the past this isn't sport or amusement or imprisonment.

This is preservation. This is apology. All remaining animals have been protected for preservation. For veneration. For so, so much apology.

It is from here that woodland wildlife like squirrels, chipmunks, raccoons, and various birds have been introduced to the greenspaces belting the City on I-285 and crossing that belt on I-20. Our scientists and engineers have balanced our air and climate systems within the Dome, and over the last couple decades the entrance to our ecosystem of non-human life has been carefully prepared and arranged.

We passed the house cat enclosure and I tried not to linger and succumb to distraction, but the eyes of the City's lone tabby, Mister Fuffles, always hooked me. They were a deep green, like some damp ancient mountain bog I'd seen at the image-bank. Even peripherally they caught me. The silent orange cat stared into me and suddenly I was bold.

"I'm sorry to disturb your process, Detective Rabbinowitz, but I'm curious. Is that 'Zoo Zoo Jupiter' you are humming? I thought I heard it back at Delphi also," I asked.

There was a moment on his face of such seriousness, as he emerged from his investigatory mode of awareness, that I was truly frightened I had offended him. That this relationship was damaged, if not ended.

Then he took a breath and smiled at me in recognition, as if newly aware of my presence.

"Ha, um, it is actually that melody, but I was singing 'Jew Jew Zupiter,'" and he explained to me that as a child he latched onto the song. He was mentally slow and physically weak. His confused mind, not yet focused, chattered the lyrics into easy first consonant sound substitution. As he learned about his faith and the faith of his family part of the nonsense stood out and song became a mantra as he did what he could to build up his mind and body before admittance to the SunSpot Cyborg Program.

Now it is the perfect rememory to prove his own humanity back to himself. The fact that he once created something so silly. Something purely non-utilitarian. Something pure. Something that now ironically serves a purpose. For all the sharpening, honing, and hewing of his focus. For all the gaming his mind and body through the cyborg enhancements. For all the dedication to the City and his work, he rarely has the chance to wonder at what cost it has all come. Then there is "Jew Jew Zupiter" and he knows who he is.

After his explanation we passed through a misty amphibian enclosure and facilitators were making tadpoles comfortable for their metamorphoses. It appeared Thinkowitz was being careful in his footwork to walk abreast of me, with me, instead of a few feet ahead, leading in his own world.

We stopped at a facilitator who told us his name was Elliot Ulysses. He showed us a frog mid-metamorphoses. It was otherwise a tadpole. A black, bulbous, wet thing. But legs of another identity had burst forth to flank its slender tail. I felt an awe at a true form of magic happening before me. An awe akin to what I heard from those who delivered testimonials about the Oracle.

"It's like magic," I couldn't hold back.

"It very much is, Casaubon," said Thinkowitz. He thanked Elliot Ulysses and still by my side, led us out of the sticky enclosure and onto the open path.

"I think you are right for this work, Casaubon. You have humility and a sense of openness that is very useful when investigating the Sacred," he said.

We were walking on a little bridge over dry terrain where snakes roamed and explored. We were talking. I'm sure my partner was still using most of his awareness and mental faculties to scan for what was not present, but otherwise we were walking and talking at the Zoological Sanctuary together.

"A writer of the early 20th century described Modernity as a state—or inducing a state of disenchantment. He used the German word, *entzauberung*, which literally means 'de-magic-action.' With the death of that mono-god of Modernity we are re-enchanted, magic has returned to the world. With the RESURGA we are re-enchanted. Through our re-enchantment we heal. What you felt looking at the tadpole in transition is a connection to truth and a connection to mystery. Feeling the harmony of both is the benefit of our world," and as he spoke, he pointed out a soft, torn, empty shell that once housed an unborn snake.

As we rounded west towards the middle lawn of the Sanctuary, we heard the barking and saw the pure joy of canines at play. The City preserved a small collection to the delight of all citizens. There was once such a time of darkness before the RESURGA when watching such animals bound and play was inconceivable.

Taking everything in, I listened as Thinkowitz continued.

"Without Kapital we need to have some sort of devotional abstraction. And since we have unlimited energy and no material worries, we fill our time with religious zeal. I understand that your faith is the hardest to find joy within. I imagine that is why Profane Safety was the obvious path. You're Sacred now though," he said.

Thinkowitz then explained that his function is to transcend the divide between the two: Sacred and Profane. His god is just as fantastical as Cthulhu and his role in his job, like the role of City Safety on the whole, is to root in reason the fantastical tendency of humans, its citizens. He does that within himself as a rational theist, an oxymoronic statement.

"We have learned with a trial by fire and water, a trial of destruction, that the danger of an all-encompassing abstraction is real, that the god Kapital became too strong when believed *en masse*. It is the problem of monotheism. I admit now to be a henotheist, as Abraham himself was. As was Moses," he said, and continued:

"The final prophet of the god of Islam writes in Surah 109 of the Qur'an, *I worship not that which you worship, nor will you worship that which I worship. And I shall not worship that which you are worshipping. Nor will you worship that which I worship. To you be your religion, and to me my religion.* The title of this Surah is often translated as 'Unbelievers.' It is the most civil way to manage a society. Henotheism based out of tolerance and a mutual respect of difference. Here we are all believers, even those Abyssoids who believe in nothing."

Up around the goat enclosure we strolled and approaching Meiko Ran we halted our conversation.

She pointed out the small ensemble of goats, bounding and chewing and butting. We noticed the absence of Mac. Then we continued to stroll.

The kind teacher, a rabbi always, Thinkowitz resumed his lesson as we passed an enclosure where beavers were building a tall lodge of felled sticks and logs.

"Kapital was at once the Tower of Babel and the smiting god at its top. Like how Tartarus is both place and deity. The poly-symphonic worshipful voices in the City, that stirring cacophony that seems like chaos to you, Casaubon, is the veritable harmony of humanity. Due to my enhancement I can listen at any point like the center of a storm with big ears. I was engineered for this work. But you have a natural affinity, it seems," he said and stopped walking.

I didn't want to stop listening, but I was ready for anything.

"A red herring?" he asked me.

"Do you want to do a reconnaissance of the aquatic enclosure," I asked.

Then laughter. So much deep, sincere laughter. The bearded man in all black, a man who knew everything and had just been applauding my aptitude at doing work he has devoted his whole life to was laughing. And he was laughing at me.

"No, Casaubon. Our lead. The reason for our walk in the park today. The excuse for a stroll and conversation during a troubling investigation. Is MacAvoy a red herring?"

And it was just then, while standing at the north end of the Zoological Sanctuary, that Meiko Ran messaged us. The goat had been found. And alive.

Apparently, MacAvoy was as good at hiding as she was at jumping.

"She was napping in some bushes..." I related before I was cut off.

"Behind the amphibian enclosure?" interrupted my partner. And he was right.

Then Detective Rabbi Jakob Rabbinowitz said to me, "At least this investigation didn't turn out to be a tragedy. Literally."

I asked him what he meant.

"In attic Greek, the original meaning of the word 'tragedy' is 'goat song,' from the word *tragos*, meaning 'he-goat,' and *aeidein*, which means to sing; the same root as the word 'ode.' One theory is that the first Greek dramatic songs of suffering were sung around the sacrifice of a goat. Alas, sadly our song is sung around a much more profound loss," he said with a somber grimace and sad, smiling eyes.

...And That is That

Wednesday, I ventured out into the night to walk with purpose and direction.

After I left work earlier, I made a side trip on my way home. The home of Juani Negra was up in Brookhaven. Messaging ahead, he was alone when I arrived, no Uco Azul. I was relieved. The thought of seeing them both was too much for me. He was gracious and happy for me to take some of his home brewed pulque with nothing in exchange.

I went home and showered and changed into clothes so light they barely touched my body. They fell around me and down me with gentle draping and with each step moved a breath ahead.

Even though I had a direction and the trams are fast, when I left home, I journeyed by foot to ground. I didn't want to feel contained. Or at the whim of the tram. I needed to cover my own terrain.

The pulque was in a plant-plastic sack slung over my shoulder on my back. It bounced with my steps, not yet a jog, but undeniably a bustle. I would relax in the right place and time.

East at McClendon. Then Howard Circle all the way to Wisteria Way and on into Oakhurst.

The building was a contemporary design, *natural rebirth*, and abound with floral touches. The center of the structure reached Dome-ward over sixty stories. Off the center structure budded each apartment.

I took the lift up to the thirtieth floor. The door of the first apartment on the right was left ajar in expectation of my arrival.

The music that welcomed me wasn't familiar, but it was nice. Ivy Andermatt was walking across her apartment holding two earthenware cups with ancient Sumerian designs and heading for her porch. She gestured for me to follow.

"Did you bring the pulque?" she asked as we got comfortable on our own divans and looked out at the City. The City was alive and beautiful, like my friend.

We drank and I enjoyed a late in the day mind away. Uco Azul was very correct about his friend's pulque. It burned down my throat like smooth fire and every dark hair on my body stood up in its follicle.

I didn't want to talk about my day. So, I let my friend do all of the talking. At first it was nice to just lay back and drink and listen. But soon the pulque made my lips numb and finger tips tingly and my listening became less idle.

Ivy Andermatt told me about her deity. She spoke like she was deeply in love.

Her words described a system where no one is forgotten, abandoned, or left out. Her goddess, like Hecate, or the Roman god, Janus, whose month it was, guarded a threshold. It was *the* threshold through which all will pass. But Ninedinna is no mere usher. She records every name, codifying and canonizing every identity when the identity is concluded. An inventory of the dead is an inventory of all who have lived.

"Regardless of who you are or what you've done. Regardless of how insignificant you might feel, Ninedinna honors everyone equally," she said

"You know so much," I replied, a captivated listener.

"It's part of my practice of my faith. For her, for Ninedinna, the Goddess of Names of the Dead, I must record. I honor her through my work as an archivist and let her guide my hand," she said.

"I want to ask you so much more about your goddess. And how it feels to have a goddess with you while you work. I'm always investigating. I'm sorry. And I must be the dullest person you know. You know all about my god. Everyone does."

She leaned in and kissed me to cheer me up. I kissed back.

She asked me if sex would be a good way to enhance my calm, a good break from the investigation.

I smiled and told her that I believed she had the right idea. We left the balcony and went inside.

A few hours later we finished the pulque and then she cheered me up again. I felt seen, known, and acknowledged.

CHANT OF THE EVER CIRCLING SKELETAL FAMILY

Doubt was starting to creep in.

I worried that we might never know anything. Maybe I shouldn't have taken a break last night? It was nice though. And I rested. And slept.

There was no possibility that my partner's mind would rest though. That beyond the cyborg enhancements of his brain power and capacity, his will, his "Jew Jew Zupiter" drive, would not allow the murder of Tiresias Pythia to remain unsolved.

I didn't see him at City Safety headquarters today and I came home early. It is not my place to check up on him, so I waited.

And then he called. No message. A call.

"Casaubon! I have been thinking about our visit to the City Sovereign and his wife," began Thinkowitz, excited or agitated or even joyous. I couldn't tell. I had yet to experience him like this.

"But his possible motive doesn't hold much weight. You agreed," I responded.

"Yes, yes, correct, correct. It's not about promoting the Cyborg Program. And the obsidian in the throat looks so unplanned, so sudden. If this was premeditated wouldn't the killer have brought their own weapon? Unless they were a frequent visitor and knew about the obsidian. Remember Aristotle. Remember William of Ockham. The method looks unplanned and most likely it is. The barest appearance of reality here is that someone heard something they didn't like. Something so awful it drove them to kill," he said.

"So, what have you been thinking about from our visit?" I asked.

"They were nervous. They seemed guilty. However, that is not an indicator of much in our sullen utopia. It was when he spoke of those final days of Dome construction. Some of his words stood out to me. They have crawled across my mind. It is difficult to describe. They have sparked unconnected associations. It took some time to figure out how to treat them...

"The word that stood out the most was sacrifice. He used it many times. All in regard to that time, but another word of his made it stranger. Family. But plural. He mentioned sacrifice and families. 'We must honor them,' he said. 'The sacrifices that families made,' he said. And he was talking about back then. Back when he was a child. A child without a family. An orphan. Why would he dwell on the sacrifice families made when he was an orphan?" he asked and I hoped it was rhetorical.

I had no idea where he was going with all of this, but at this point my job was to support him.

"So, I went to see your friend in City Safety Records, Ivy Andermatt, the worshipper of Ninedinna. She does quite commendable work. Files are thorough and very detailed. All testimonials of the those who lived through the Katastrophe are logged. She has made this effort for the last years of Dome construction, that darkness before the dawn of final RESURGA."

I smiled at her name and felt a shared pride in Ivy's fastidiousness.

"There was a great amount of information to go through, but I turned my focus on the file compiled about Spendeva Luna. She was a child during the worst years of transition out of Katastrophe and into RESURGA. While the Dome was being completed and safety was on the horizon the reactions of the populace were wide-ranging.

"It was a time of street prophets on every corner. Itinerant ecstatics roamed wherever they could find an audience. There were messages of hope and there were panics of despair. Spendeva had lost her parents by age fourteen and was on her own. She was traveling with a boyfriend not much older than her and at fifteen gave birth.

"We know all of this because she was interviewed by a social worker at the dawn of the RESURGA. This was during the first RESURGA census. Living on the streets, from one haphazard shelter to the next during this time of great upheaval was very rough on her. Sharing a shelter with other scavengers and street prophets while caring for her new baby, she was approached by an ecstatic and a prophecy was thrust upon her. Maybe they didn't want to share the space and supplies with an infant. Maybe they were just crazy or cruel. Regardless, Spendeva Luna was told:

This baby will be the death of you and his father. You want him as an act of hope, but he will fuck your hope. He will fuck you... fuck you up.

"This is what she told the social worker verbatim. What she claims she was told verbatim. So, she left the baby on the doorstep of the closest orphanage. She notes that the father did die anyway. Years later of radiation poisoning while working on the Dome. She calls the Dome a curse more than a salvation. The interviewing social worker took this all down while diagnosing her trauma and helped her find work in the RESURGA.

"Spendeva Luna became a zealous and active citizen of the City. She assumed the child had died. Infant mortality was at the highest recorded numbers before the Dome was completed. City orphanages were pediatric morgues. She worked hard against the guilt of her sacrifice.

"Eventually she met Ped Malus. When they married, she told him she lost a child before the Dome was completed. She never wanted one again, never wanted to feel that loss again. It was fine with him. He lived for the City. She gave her child up for the City. Now they lived for it together.

"Your friend's records are very thorough. She honors her goddess well. In my brain I compiled then cross-referenced all orphanage records for that time period and region of the City. The baby lived and the City raised that child, Casaubon."

Then Thinkowitz told me that he called the Sovereign and informed him that we know what happened and are on our way. I needed to meet him at the tram stop closest to my building right now.

But the last thing he said before that reverberated in my head:

The baby lived and the City raised that child, Casaubon.

LAZARUS

"How could they know. It was just a story they were telling me. But I felt it's truth."

He stood there trembling before us and the City down below.

The same office and quarters in Peachtree Towers where we interviewed him before. Now in the dark, the lights off, the City casting a corona of electric light around him from behind.

"My body repulsed...

"I wanted to vomit and cry...

"And in one breath I held it all in and...

"Staring at those dead eyes. Those all-seeing dead eyes. All knowing...

"And… And I grabbed a round blackness with mass from the altar and…

"I had to shut that mouth. I had to end that story…

"But I can still hear it."

The Sovereign staggers back and gasps, clutching his ears.

"She can't hear it anymore," he groans out and points to the black touch-wall behind him.

On gesture-command it goes transparent and there in the adjoining bedroom, Spendeva Luna, his wife, his mother, supine on the bed, in the same gown of grey mesh, her lower torso and legs oozing the spent life of loose blood, two long metal hair pins standing out of jagged cuts over her uterus.

"I told her you were coming. I told her our shame would be known…

"And she did this. And I am alone…

"I am abandoned again… by her."

He ran to her and threw himself upon her.

There was nothing we could do to stop it. Before we could reach him, he was on her.

From her dead womb he drew the metal hair pins up over his head, let out a wet groaning howl, and then drove the pins deeply down through his eyes.

Life On Mars?

I took the tram to the limits: Griffin.

A giant statue of a lion's body with the head and wings of an eagle greeted me at the station. It looked serious and formidable. It reminded me of Thinkowitz.

I ambled through town and felt the sidewalk turn to sand beneath my work boots. The edge of the Dome was in the distance and I wasn't alone in being drawn to it. No one ever is.

A crowd stood before a riser. It was focused on the naked and pregnant Priestess of Nut, Egyptian goddess, who stood high before the onlookers. Her name was Divincia Dôme DuMonde and her shiny body was covered in hieroglyphs.

While I couldn't understand what she said to the crowd, they understood. They murmured with her words and their heads jerkily bowed every time she punctuated her sermon with a fist-pound against the edge of the Dome above her. They all might worship a different Dome-associated deity, but her words always drew a crowd.

For a moment she looked right at me and I felt the urge to bow my head, but instead I held her gaze until the verge of tears and then broke the look to walk away. Away from the devoted throng and the alluring spectacle of nudity, ancient text on flesh, and the glistening rotunda of her belly, I walked alone to a sharp inclining edge of the Dome.

There it was, the ocean. The sweet Vidalia Sea, specifically. It raged and steamed beyond my touch. Clouds touching waves, waves touching clouds, evaporation and precipitation passing back and forth in a continuous process only disrupted by lightning. The lightning was a constant. As constant as the plastic detritus in the waves.

No wonder the people of Griffin worshiped the Dome. It keeps them safe. It is their god. That which is always just past it is the dark alternative.

We, in our Dome, must look like colonists on our own planet. It does not welcome us anymore and we cannot live free of the world of humankind.

I was touching the boundary of our world and it didn't matter that where my eyes fell I could not go without a protective suit. We live in a world where the weather never changes. And yet in the world just beyond our sky-window the weather never stops changing. We tint gasses within the layers of the Dome at night for a sense of calm. With your face pressed this close there is no calm.

The beach glittered with what looked like stars but were only shimmering shards of new glass, lightning-quickened sand. Plastics raked across the false stars and returned to their home with the pull of the waves.

Visiting the boundary between our world and that other world, a world that might be more *the real world* than our own, is necessary for mental health. But even here and now, touching the limit, it can still feel like watching a film through a screen.

I am that girl with the mousy hair, just like in the song that became an anthem during the RESURGA. It began ironically, to cover the fears of the hopeful, fears that it wouldn't work, that the Dome wouldn't hold. But there was no going to Mars, we're here still, we're alive, and Bowie is a Profane Prophet held on high.

Along with him, there is always Whitman in my head: *Sea of stretch'd ground-swells, Sea breathing broad and convulsive breaths, Sea of the brine of life and of unshovell'd yet always ready graves.* Walt would weep to see this. But he would be proud of what we have built inside the Dome.

We aren't perfect though.

Poor Tiresias Pythia. Poor Ped Malus. Poor Spendiva Luna. It was always a tragedy, just like she said.

My partner has a deep commitment to religious belief as well as mystery and its value in our lives, but that does not work in opposition to material truths of this world. *How did they know*, the Sovereign asked at the end? I'm sure he asked that every moment after he forced the obsidian into the Oracle's throat. My partner placed all attribution on the cyborg enhancements. Tiresias Pythia collected and collated data in a similar fashion to his own process. They assembled truth by finding connections in disparate sources. They gave those truths back and told each seeker what they wanted, or what they needed, to hear.

"This does not discount their role as a prophet though," he said. "In *The Guide for the Perplexed*, Rabbi Moses Ben Maimon tells us, 'Prophecy is, in truth and reality, an emanation sent forth by God through the medium of the Active Intellect: first to one's rational faculty and then to one's imaginative faculty. It is the highest degree and greatest perfection humans can attain.' My god works in mysterious ways. Working through a cyborg enhancement is not even *that* mysterious."

The Sovereign and his wife had both left detailed funerary arrangements. We worked late into the night Thursday to complete the investigation and finally inter their bodies in Tartarus by dawn.

Yesterday was the funeral procession for Tiresias Pythia, the Oracle of Delphi. Their body was carried in a clear plant-plastic preservation tube from City Safety Headquarters on Ponce west to Peachtree Street and then north to Tartarus. Thousands were in the streets wailing terrible wails and chanting joyous rhymes. Regardless of mythos, the Oracle of Delphi was revered and loved by more people now than ever.

Thinkowitz and I took a tram to observe from above and then met the Oracle at their destination. The body of Tiresias Pythia surfed up the stone steps on the tips of outstretched hands to the front door of Tartarus where N'Deye Frimbo waited to receive his friend.

Today was my partner's holy day and he has been resting. Tonight, I will meet him at The Earl.

RaMBaM, Thank You, Ma'am

The Brothers Panic had just finished "Sense of Doubt" with hopeful major chords, chirping, and wind.

Sacred Detective Rabbi Jakob "Thinkowitz" Rabbinowitz was sipping a plum wine produced in small batches in the back of The Earl. Indecisive about celebratory inebriants and ever the dutiful disciple, I ordered the same and followed his sip with my own.

We sat at a table in the front row, but off to the side near the bar. The place was crowded with mourners and listeners at every table and filling all standing room. Anne-Locke and Suzy each took turns to check on us and thank us for our work. They knew the Oracle, and they were regular visitors.

"Hail, and hello, again everyone for coming and..." said Max or Jack, and the other:

"...out of sadness and respect and love and devotion..." said the other and then:

"...and remembrance, so much remembrance, and more love..." said the original speaker, and then:

"...this next song is for the holiest of prophets we have never known, they who spoke for and through..." said the other, and then:

"...the great god Apollo, god of truth, light, reason, and music..." said the first speaker, and then:

"...and so for Tiresias Pythia, the Oracle of Delphi, this is..." said the other, and then:

"... 'Weeping Wall'..." and then they both turned to their keyboard and touch table and began.

The Brothers Panic wore only fluffy fur-looking loincloths similar to our prior interaction. While they performed, they were mellow and focused. All of their manic energy channeled into respecting the purity of each note and sound.

The song was stirring. I had never heard it live before. I gave myself over to it as it seemed my partner had, but where his dour façade and focus now allowed a sweet smile, I was weeping.

When the song ended, I asked my partner, "Detective Rabbinowitz, is this our goat song?"

"Yes, my dear Casaubon, and our work is a goat song. For as the *Book of Ecclesiastes* tells us, 'Whatever task comes your way, do it with all of your might; because in Sheol, where you will go, there is no work, no planning, no wisdom, nor knowledge,' and please, feel free to call me, Thinkowitz, if you'd like. You've earned it."

My report is also a goat song. The sacrifice was a great one for this world, but we are no strangers to sacrifice. Through so much pain and loss, we continue with our Somber-Hope, but it is a hope nonetheless.

Tip my report to the left on its side and see our jagged skyline of towers and pylons. You can draw the connected Dome across the top. To you, the future, this was my world. Maybe it was yours too. Or maybe you've done better than us.

Acknowledgements

As always in writing a book, there are many people to thank.

Firstly, my appreciation for Nate Ragolia and Shaunn Grulkowski of Spaceboy Books knows no bounds. Those beautiful demi-gods gave me a contract for this book based solely on a very long and zealous description in a Facebook message. I love you both!

Sam Grant, who created the gorgeous image on the cover, who I've known since college, is a true visionary on paper and on film. Thank you for evoking my art through yours, Sam!

Muriel Call, a sweet human and admirable reader, did me the kindness of an early read with notes. Praise Agusaya and Mr. Fluffles, Muriel!

Brook Atkinson gave my children the love and attention during the last month of writing that allowed me to rest my worry and do my work. May you be thanked in many more books, Brook!

And then there's the family and friends: Ariane and Clint (and John and Catherine); Jon and Emily Polk (and Ada and Agnes); Gail Polk; Travis and Susie Burch; Tanya and Andy Frazee (and Cecilie); William T. Vollmann; Brian and Anna Grace (and Greta); Mike Karczewski; Matt and Shawn McKinney; Neil Graf;

Mike Petri and Tara Biamby (and Liam); Kristin Hood; Bill and Crystal Brandon (and Quentin and Greyson); Molly Williams; Nick and Erin Maulding; Mark Hewitt and Fiona Reardon; Faisal Khan; Kai Reidl; Melissa Leahy; Adrienne and Amy Gandolfi; Adam Shprintzen; Ian Campbell; Elizabeth Weintraub; Rachel McDonald; Christopher Nelms; Kim Kirby and Benji Barton; Sharmeen and César Herdandez; Bobbi Jo Clarke; Carol and Jason Laws; Carolyn Christ; and Miles Liebtag. I'd be dead without y'all.

And my teachers: Van Hartmann, Peter Gardella, Carolyn Medine, Joel Black, and Thomas Cerbu. What y'all have taught me I still carry.

And literary kinfolk: Pam Jones, Jeff Jackson, Erika T. Wurth, Joanna C. Valente, Duncan Barlow, Darius James, James Reich, Reginald McKnight, Jarett Kobek, and Chris Kelso. Y'all inspire me.

And thank you to Jessica, Fox, and Søren: my heart embodied thrice.

About the Author

Jordan A. Rothacker is a writer who lives in Athens, Georgia where he received a MA in Religion and a PhD in Comparative Literature from the University of Georgia. He also received a BA in Philosophy from Manhattanville College in Purchase, New York, the state in which he was born. His essays, reviews, interviews, poetry, and fiction have been featured in such publications as *The Exquisite Corpse*,

The author as Tarot "Magician" by photographer Ben Rouse

Guernica, *Bomb Magazine*, *Entropy*, *Vol. 1 Brooklyn*, *Brooklyn Rail*, *Rain Taxi*, *Dead Flowers*, *Literary Hub*, and *The Believer*. Rothacker is the author of the novels: *The Pit, and No Other Stories* (Black Hill Press, 2015); *And Wind Will Wash Away* (Deeds, 2016); and *My Shadow Book by Maawaam* (Spaceboy Books, 2017); and the short story collection, *Gristle: weird tales* (Stalking Horse Press, 2019). 2021 will see Rothacker's first non-fiction collection, *Dead Letters: Epitaphs, Encomia, and Influence* (Reprobate Books).

For publishing news visit jordanrothacker.com.

About the Publishing Team

Nate Ragolia was labeled as "weird" early in elementary school, and it stuck. He's a lifelong lover of science fiction, and a nerd/geek. In 2015 his first book, *There You Feel Free*, was published by 1888's Black Hill Press. He's also the author of *The Retroactivist*, published by Spaceboy Books. He founded and edits BONED, an online literary magazine, has created webcomics, and writes whenever he's not playing video games or petting dogs.

Shaunn Grulkowski has been compared to Warren Ellis and Phillip K. Dick and was once described as what a baby conceived by Kurt Vonnegut and Margaret Atwood would turn out to be. He's at least the fifth best Slavic-Latino-American sci-fi writer in the Baltimore metro area. He's the author of *Retcontinuum,* and the editor of *A Stalled Ox* and *The Goldfish,* among others.